MOUNTAINS OF SMOKE

Frank Duffy

GALLOWS
PRESS

MOUNTAINS OF SMOKE

© 2013 Frank Duffy
Trade Paperback Edition

ISBN-13: 978-0615880280
ISBN-10: 0615880282

Published by
GALLOWS PRESS 2013
Moosup, Ct. 06354

Cover, Interior Design, and Typesetting
© Tom Moran

Stock photos © CanStockPhoto

Editing
Tori Crumb , Billie Moran

www.gallowspress.com

TABLE OF CONTENTS

MOUNTAINS OF SMOKE

(1)

People often ask why I write the things I do, why I abandoned the less manifest, but quietly reputable niche of drama for that of the much derided horror genre. They want to know how I could write something as successfully dank as The River Place? One of my earlier readers even emailed to me to say why she'd no longer be buying any of my other dread fantasies as she put it. Such madness within those pages, I'll pray for you.

I'd like to tell them it's a remorseless love which drives me, or at least a mutilated facsimile of it, a primitive compulsion that makes me do things unpalatable even as thoughts. But most of all it's the loneliness which has propelled me this far, a lifelong seclusion spent writing in the darkness with only my thoughts for company. My critics say I'm the archetypal writer with pretensions, that I've willingly cast myself out, duly exorcising any nonsensical ideas of literary grandeur I may have once coveted. Perhaps.

I remember telling a guest something similar, completely undeterred by their paralysis and inability to voice their response, their frightened eyes fluttering uncontrollably as the drugs invaded their bloodstream, I added that necessity had made me do these things. And once I realized how much I enjoyed slipping the pills into their drinks, tiny egg-shaped capsules like beautiful chemical depth charges, dissolving my guilt as they dissolve undetected, I would finally whisper to them of the miracle of resurrection.

(2)

We bought Rock Hill back when Jack's hair was still the color of his mother's. The critics were perilously close to fawning at my feet, and Lana had only just finished her second novel. When I first saw the house it reminded me of a ruined castle I'd once seen while hiking with some university friends through the Czech Republic. Like those medieval remains Rock Hill looked built for defense. Three storey's high, with mossy stone walls, its roof surrounded by the jagged lines of railings, it stood over the river as if expecting hostilities from afar. A wrought iron balcony extended from the third floor, and sets of wooden shutters were fastened over the windows. Lana said it made her think of a house in a story about ghosts, but she couldn't remember the name of the title and we spent the best part of the return journey playfully arguing over what might have been imaginary.

(3)

It was Colin Keyes, my loyal and astute editor, who told us about Rock Hill. The house had belonged to a Hollywood film producer with whom Colin had been negotiating with over the rights to a book by one of his newest authors.

"He's decamped to England for less calamitous business climes," he told me over the phone, "and he's got this big house you might want to take a look at. And when I say big I mean big." Colin told me the producer had inherited it from a great aunt he'd never met, that despite its parochial charms it was too European in its Dickensian bleakness for his Los Angeles sensitivities.

It was a two hour drive from the city, out in the middle of the country. We drove through small villages with old farms dotting the horizon as they withered in the heat like museum pieces. We passed stone clad churches, Norman buildings, their graveyards tangled in the sun beneath juniper trees. We had the windows wound down so Jack could see more clearly the landscape of yellow hay bales, cottages and old people on bicycles.

On arriving we held our collective breath in admiration, for there it stood, Rock Hill, a grand and hefty slab of architecture which would soon be our new home even if we hadn't said so yet. It dominated the hillside and the river below, the smiles on our faces wider than the bright arc of the sun as it crested along horizon. We stopped the car at the open gates and watched Jack run up the overgrown driveway to the house.

"Do you think it'll mind the company?" Lana asked, that regal frown of hers disturbing the spray of freckles on her cheeks.

"It probably hasn't had a family in there since God knows when," I said.

"It looks as if it might resent the intrusion, " she said.

I waited for her to smile, to dismiss her words as having little or no meaning, but she continued to stare at the house, watching our son run up the driveway as if to a grandparent awaiting his return.

(4)

We threw a housewarming party for close family and friends. It was July, but it rained that day, so most of our time was spent indoors inventing puerile forms of entertainment. The kids loved it as we chased one other in drunken relay races through its many rooms, Jack with his older cousins positioned on the landings as arbitrary judges, all of whom screamed with laughter at our stupidity, thinking all the adults had gone mad.

When I actively picture that day I think of Lana and Uncle Trevor colliding on the bend of the second floor corridor as they raced to grab a bar of chocolate the kids had hidden in the large cracked pot for Jack's cactus. I think of my cousin Arnold stooped over Aunt Sylvia's cashmere jumper thrown over one arm of the sofa, vomiting the contents of the half bottle of wine he'd drunk earlier. I think of Colin Keyes proclaiming my new novel, 'The Dark Coldness Of Arthur Hoyle' a classic in the making.

"Only it needs a little more violence, though a little less authentic," he slurred, slugging shots of tequila as if he'd never encountered alcohol in all his forty-three years of entertaining authors.

Rock Hill, it infected everyone, drove them silly with admiration.

(5)

The house leans out from an outcrop of limestone over the river and sandy marshes, an awkward looking lighthouse, a misplaced landmark out here in the deathly calm of the countryside, only that slash of tumultuous water lending it credibility. Lana once told me we were incredibly lucky with Rock Hill, but as the lights from the upper windows go out once more of their own accord, making fun of the shadows, I think she meant something altogether different. For out there in the coldness of the river there is frenzied movement a churning slap dash in the water. An owl hoots from the trees on the other side of the river, a car drives over the bridge, its lights trickling in reflections and a drowned memory comes dragging itself through the marsh and weeds, its face staring up at me, merciless and unyielding.

(6)

We filled the house with the kind of furniture we'd always wanted, antique clocks, expensive prints for the hallways and corridors, mahogany tables, saddle brown rugs, satin curtains, brass molded worktops in the gargantuan kitchen and original timber beams crisscrossing its ceiling. We had the garden landscaped, with fir saplings riding the freshly interred turf on the west side and a low rock wall lining the east side, the lawn sloping down the center towards the top of the rock face, cordoned off by a twelve foot high fence. Below you could watch the river racing along, its green fronds whispering beneath the surface. I told Jack it was the hair of drowned sailors.

(7)

In summer evenings when everybody was asleep, I'd sit on the lawn watching the river. My thoughts were like the shapeless flotsam that scudded its surface, and like anything that isn't moored or tied down they'd become endless islands of incongruous substance, my mind turning in dizzying cycles towards half-realized denouncements and wayward plot deviations I'd yet to solve. Eventually I'd get up and walk back to the house, marveling at its sheer size and suddenly the need to compose one more fiction wouldn't seem so important. For ten years we lived there as strong and happy as any family we knew, where arguments raged and where the subsequent conciliations forged themselves as if willed by the house. It was there we wrote our favorite books, lived our lives passionately and loved one another with the fiercest of loyalties.

(8)

My visitors come to Rock Hill to ask their meaningless questions, to sit in my house and contentedly stir their drinks, some of them smoking, some of them not, thinking they can see into me, thinking they can pry me out from the stone under which they think I've crawled. They believe themselves to be sensitive souls, philosophically entertaining my revival at their hands. Such a tasteless and discouraging psychology. They want only confirmation that my wife's death has catapulted me from one literary darkness straight into another. It make sense to them, an understandable tidiness requiring very little thought. I've no qualms about mixing them their drinks and watching them slide away into another of my coldly engineered sleepovers.

(9)

It was the week before Christmas and Lana had just finished a meeting with her editor about her sixth novel. It was her best yet, and naturally we were all excited. She came out of the publishers, no doubt brimming with good thoughts, and slipped on a patch of ice on the steps to the main entrance. She hit the pavement hard, fracturing her skull in two places, as if aiming for some kind of perfect symmetry to her injuries. They rushed her to the city hospital, but she never regained consciousness, not even when Jack stood at her bedside in the intensive care unit sobbing, not even when I sat at the foot of the bed cracking a string of her favorite jokes, believing that somehow the memory of their idiocy might open a door into the world in which she'd vanished without warning. I had only to look at her face, at the faint pulse of life behind her closed eyes to know she'd shut down as the machine to which the doctors had attached her would itself soon stop working.

I remember Lana once describing to some magazine journalist conducting an interview over the phone that death was for her like: 'waltzing off into a permanent refuge from which one is exempt the more mundane stuff of adulthood.' The write-up in the next issue of the magazine gave us plenty to laugh about because she hadn't meant a word, only saying those things to get rid of the journalist. Naturally I hated her for ever having uttered any such thing, even in jest, for now it seemed this was her punishment for making light of the interviewer's questions.

(10)

I leave the package on the rock some twenty feet below the broken hole in the fence. There is a moon again, but ersatz, ill defined. The river is black because of it, a solid arrow shot towards the Atlantic ocean, always in flight. There is a snuffling sound coming from below, like a dog with its nose to the door as it scents the smell of something or somebody on the other side. The moon glows briefly, the marshland lit, a landscape of undulations and spiked mounds, and I can see the undressed corpse and the dark figure bent over it chewing at its face.

(11)

I remember the doctors and nurses streaming out of a room with curtains like the gauze bandages they carried with them.

The failure of the operation confirmed what I'd known the second I'd looked at her in the hospital bed, her and with it the constant flow of activity ceased like a heartbeat trace on a monitor.

Jack found me in the corridor outside the intensive care unit. Julia Albright was with him, Lana's closest friend and illustrator for the publishing house which had bought her first novel. I looked at the pair of them but said hardly anything. I'd no time for selfless acts of comfort. Julia tried talking to me, but all I remember was her ring encrusted hand on my shoulder and a huge leather bag drooping from her jeweled wrist, unimportant details which for some reason hold a vaster significance than the expression on Jack's face at that time.

"Do something, dad," Jack said. He was eighteen years old, a young man with an old head and a good heart, but fear and the impending finality of grief made him resemble a child.

"Be quiet, son, please."

He raced away up the corridor with Julia staggering after him in her expensive shoes. The only thing I felt was relief, and maybe fleetingly disgust at my behavior.

Three days later a nurse with an understanding expression let me into the same room after the doctors had left for the last time. I stood over Lana's body, but for some reason I couldn't think of anything to say. An orderly came in and gave me a plastic carrier bag with her possessions, saying how very sorry he was for my loss and left me thinking thoughts I hardly care to acknowledge. Like some scavenging animal I emptied the contents of the bag onto the floor, curls of yellow receipts, tubes of countless lip balms, scattering them under the bed, ransacking her possessions for clues as to the puzzle of her death.

(12)

I spent the evening in a bar near the hospital, looking out the window as if expecting Lana to walk past unencumbered by the constraints that death brings. Despite my patience she never showed. I started a fight with a man I'd seen in A & E the day before when I was passing through to the elevator for the intensive care ward. Somehow the fight ended up outside in a deserted car-park, and one punch sent me sprawling over a stand of gas cylinders, which unfortunately didn't explode into scorching garlands of fire.

Later the two us shared a bottle of whiskey on the curb of the street, trading war stories. Only at the end when the man climbed into a taxi and said he was sorry, did I tell him about my wife. I don't remember his name, but I recall quite clearly as he was getting into the taxi that he hugged me and said he was sorry.

(13)

The day of the funeral, in the middle of the wake, I told Lana's parents I was through with writing. I didn't explain what that meant. And neither did they ask. I suspect they thought I would return to it one day.

(14)

Lana once described what we did as the equivalent of attempting to scale mountains as intangible as smoke. At the time I'd thought she meant writing, which can often be so indefinably out of reach that simply getting it down on paper feels like an act of complete insanity. Now I realize she hadn't meant that at all.

13

(15)

I'm beyond them now, and most likely they will soon be so far out of reach it would be as if I'd never known them. I wrote that two weeks after Lana's death. I wrote it with a cigarette in my hand, having returned to the vice at my wife's wake. It felt good to breath in the acridity of the smoke, like inhaling it meant scouring my lungs of anything worth saving, the capacity to fill myself up with yet more anguish, driven out by the swirling, expanding cigarette smoke.

(16)

After New Year I made the decision to send Jack back to university. I convinced him he needed his friends, not the angry widower who'd vanished for the darker climes of his imagination. But when he went without much of a protest, it naturally took me by surprise. My hypocrisy had gone unnoticed, my contradictions unheard. I'd tried giving him signs, clues, but there was no longer any Lana to translate, no mother to unscramble the confusion of our words. I drove him to the train station in the town ten miles out, bought him his ticket and angrily left him standing on the platform for Newcastle. I drove out of the station and stopped to look back. I could see him staring into the space of himself. I turned the car around, but when I ran onto the platform the train had already come and gone. An elderly woman sitting on a bench watched me intently as I headed for the exit, disdain spreading over her old face.

Back at Rock Hill I wandered the house, drinking heavily, searching for something unnamable, just as I'd searched through Lana's possessions in the hospital. But the rooms were empty, not of physical objects, but of her presence. Some of the rooms she'd hardly spent any time in at all, but what remained of the atmosphere was significantly bereft. I analyzed my thoughts, bitterly amused by my clichés, my descriptive powers already on the wane. Her death had robbed me of my one talent and I wondered if she'd ghost written my work by simply being who she was. Fascinated by this unexpected development so soon after her death I continued roaming the house, a nomadic but domesticated caretaker intent on climbing inside the roaring din that existed within the pulsing chamber of my skull.

(17)

My hangover was sufficiently monstrous on waking. I instantly reached for the second of the two half liter whisky bottles on the desktop and shakily emptied the last of it into a coffee mug, the tall glass I'd been drinking from the previous day lying in pieces on the study floor.

I stood in the middle of the room in a t-shirt and a pair of boxer shorts, my clothes twisted round each other on the sofa bed, trying to recall what I'd been doing the night before. My laptop was still on, and I scrolled down the screen to find I'd written about twenty odd pages, approximately eighteen thousand words and had even managed to give it a title: The River Place. Reading the first few lines I realized it was a horror story.

I'd grown up an aficionado of horror and weird fiction, and in my teenage years had even experimented with the genre. My study was a temple to those years, its shelves filled with books by Campbell, Aickman and Poe. How had I'd ended up walking the corridors of academia to the staged applause of resentful professors deriding my scattergun approach to prose, the boredom of having to attend such tedious ceremonies hosted by lauded wits who surveyed my work as if perusing the contents of a jumble sale?

I walked to the window from which I had a good view of the river, which on clear days it was sometimes possible to see the distant rooftops of the nearest villages. My head didn't throb but beat incessantly against my skull, and as I lifted the glass to my lips I could see there was somebody in the river idiotically attempting to swim against the current..

On top of a book shelf devoted to Algernon Blackwood was a pair of Tungsten binoculars Jack had bought me three Christmases ago. He'd obviously observed me sitting in the garden at night as I watched the river, mistakenly assuming I needed them for whatever observations he thought I might have been making. I took the binoculars back to the window expecting the person to be something else. When I realized there really was somebody in the river I felt the same overwhelming sense of panic I had the day Lana's editor had rung to tell me Lana had taken a nasty fall on the steps outside.

The person in the river looked like a woman with her long slicked back hair, tawny colored because of the dead leaves sticking to her scalp. On the river bank about thirty yards from the woman was an angler in waders knee-deep and with his back to her. I moved the binoculars to the woman again, only to realize she was naked.

It was impossible of course, the temperatures must have been enough to rob anybody of the merest chance of catching their breath, but there she was. Her head lifted for a moment and she spotted the angler, the water up to her eyes. The angler reeled his line and cast it out again, inspecting the depths, cautious, but not cautious enough to see the woman as she dived beneath the water so that only her feet visible as she kicked against the surface.

The angler must have heard her coming, for he turned to look over his shoulder as pair of hands came out of the water and grabbed him about both kneecaps, before violently yanking him down in one single movement.

(18)

By the time I made it to the car I was honest enough to admit I wasn't entirely certain of what I'd witnessed. Why was I in such a hurry to drive over to the police station? I could simply ring them and describe what I thought I'd seen, but this would probably sound a lot more crazy on the phone than it would face to face. I could hardly wait for the automatic gates to open which was why I accelerated too fast and the bumper caught the edge of the receding metal so fast the car skidded towards the track along the riverbank section. I hit the brakes and the car came to a shuddering sideways stop. I'd frightened myself enough to decide my current drunken state precluded me heading over to the police station to get myself arrested for drink driving. I climbed out of Lana's old Peugeot and sat down on the riverbank, watching the water plow mercilessly through the countryside.

(19)

On my return to the house I sat down in front of the laptop and forced myself to look at the words on the screen, that at first read like a white heat of Times New Roman, a sewage of thoughts wrapped up inside copious amounts of words and ideas that at first struggled to form any kind of cohesive narrative structure. But just as I was about to give up, several pages in, these following sentences caught my eye.

...the river, Lana, the drifting mist evaporating as she walked up onto a stretch of exposed shoreline...

...but Rock Hill, towering from its point on the hillside, vast in its own space, nullifying everything else around it...

...Lana was hungry, not only for their corpses, but for the demented architecture of his prose in which punctuation and clauses and adverbial phrases created walkways for her to escape the river...

I broke off to go downstairs to get something more to drink, the story on my lips. I didn't return to the computer for at least an hour, standing at the window overlooking the veranda, the river a grey band outlined against the glass, and wondered if Lana out there among the debris of the river?

(20)

She sits opposite me expecting something more than the story I've just finished relating to her. She has cooed her sympathies better than most, an upcoming actress of little worth, so they tell me. She is without real curiosity, purely a pretty head nodding idiotically. I switch on a lamp, one of several, one that Lana had chosen. Its halo blesses the rugs where I expect she imagines all of this will soon conclude. She had no idea such thoughts repulse me.

I tell myself it's only a matter of time before the police make the connection, but as I watch the actress bend forward to look at Lana's photograph in a frame on the coffee table, I wonder how long before the corpses wash up on the banks of the river, entangled in the novels she has inadvertently helped me create. A year has already passed, maybe they'll never make such a leap of logic.

The actress flops gracelessly across the sofa, one leg pushing the rug up with her shoeless foot. Her mouth hang open and almost immediately as she begins to snore.

(21)

The next day the news on the radio, which was playing at top volume two floors below, dragged me from my alcoholic slumber. I'd passed out next to the laptop again, and as I sat up and nudged the mouse the screen came alive with words. I'd somehow managed to write a blistering twenty thousand of them, of which I had only the slenderest memory of doing.

Was that enough for her, or did she need even more?

In my condition, sweating and shaking, the thought of going downstairs to turn off the blasted radio felt like a challenge I wasn't up for, until a fragment of the news report caught my attention. I stood up and pushed the chair back across the floor, suddenly aware of my complete nakedness. This time I'd folded my clothes into a tidy pile which I'd for some unknown reason placed on the windowsill. It was the kind of an inexplicable action only seasoned drunks are initiate enough to fully comprehend.

The walk down three flights of stairs felt as if it'd never end. There was a familiar scent in the air as I rounded each turn of the stairwell, but I thought I must have left a window open somewhere. When I reached the kitchen I saw the back door had been wedged open with a rock, a smooth and glistening cap of lichen plastered to its round body. Definitely the work of my wife. The local news report had finished but the song which had replaced it did nothing to diminish what I'd just heard: Mike Bartlett, forty-seven, father of two, missing since yesterday morning. I was certain it was the angler.

A lone cigarette sat on the edge of the draining board

miraculously untouched. I lit it off one of the cooker hobs, singeing some of the hairs on my head. Uncaring of my nakedness I opened the door wider and blew smoke into the coldness of the morning.

(22)

I took a train to meet Colin at the Eldorado near the station, the same one I'd taken Jack to shortly after Lana's funeral. I walked out of the terminal and crossed the street to the restaurant, gave my name to the maitre de who showed me to my seat. When Colin arrived he said nothing about the one empty glass of whisky being substituted for second one. I looked at the glass, shrugging half apologetically.

"I'll stop, but when I'm ready."

"I'd be the same," he said.

It'd been almost two months since the funeral. Colin was still wearing the same expression, dour, artfully controlled. He drank mineral water, his eyes following my line of sight as if afraid of where it might lead.

"I don't want to hear anything about Lana." Colin nodded, glanced away. There was a streak of grey at the left side of his temple, something I hadn't noticed before. I wondered if Lana's funeral had impacted on him more than I'd given him credit for?

I wanted a cigarette, wished I was somewhere on the continent where lightning up didn't mean attracting a thousand disapproving glances

"I have an idea for a series of books." I took a sip of my whisky, but only a sip. The previous drink had loosened me up plenty.

"What about 'All Dogs To Their Masters'?" he asked.

"Forget it."

In the ninety minutes we spent in the restaurant I couldn't remember anything about the food we ate. I do recall convincing Colin who was a non-smoker to follow me to the entrance where I had a quick cigarette on the pavement outside the entrance, before the rain drove us back to our table and a frowning maitre de.

"You make money with me, and this way I could make you a lot more."

He listened, openly astonished, before deciding he must don the professional mask and do his utmost to talk me out of it. Only he couldn't possibly hide the interested look in his eyes. He'd sometimes stop to peer at me across the table just to see if I was really being serious, eventually returning to that annoying ting he does with his fingertips as he brushes them round the rim of his glass, which I suspected was his way of trying to hypnotize himself into believing what I was telling him.

"It's not about Lana," I said, but I was lying. It was all about Lana and the facts of the matter were simple enough. Write the stories she wanted, the stories which she needed and she'd come back to me. The only problem was in finding her a regular source of food.

Back on the train I studied the faces of the other passengers, listening to their conversations. I hoped to steal a story from them, or at least the beginning of one. The River Place had reached its natural conclusion, which not even Lana could inspire to continue outside of its natural domain. Every story has an ending, no matter how abruptly or incomplete it might seem to the reader. For the writer, once they reach the end there's nothing else for them to do but move on to the next one.

(23)

Lana didn't appear that night or the following evening either. On the third day in the morning there was mist on the marshland, coming out of the forest, and I waited for it to dissolve and show my naked wife swimming her way to another unwary angler. But there were no people out there, no figures trudging the banks or the shoreline, only the wind moving the trees. In life Lana had walked into the future with no expectations but those she'd made of herself. But in death, resurrection, she was hungry for more than the story I had given her.

(24)

There's a seaside town to the north of the river. It's like any such place in winter, where its roads are mostly deserted in the evenings and only the lights in the huddled rows of pubs along its dingy high street mean life exists here at all. Through the windows of these dull facades the people roar with laughter, but these are empty gestures, ones that belie a terrible emotional sickness. I instantly recognize it. It has its own unique gravitational pull. But even more ferociously magnetic is the relentless noise the sea makes, which seems to permeate the very faces I stare at in silent understanding. And even now I can hear it, never fading.

(25)

I drove there in under an hour, which when I think about now realize was insufficient distance to put between Rock Hill and what I was planning to do. I moved from one pub to the next, drinking only coke, until I found a place next to the boarded-off pier. The pub was practically empty except for a man in a corner filling in a betting form. The barmaid paid no attention to me as I took my coke and went up to the him. He knew what I wanted before I even asked. He didn't waste time and drew me a rough map on the back of a beer matt.

I got there just as it started to rain. There were three other cars already parked up the lane, an area of wasteland nearby and a late-night off-license, ashen light creeping round the posters and cardboard in its windows. I stopped the car and a woman approached. She was middle-aged and looked painfully tired. I felt some inkling of emotion, remorse perhaps, but in the heat of my own personal needs it was barely noticeable.

Once she was sitting in the passenger seat I offered her more money to come back with me to the house. She refused at first, and I could see she wanted reassurances that I wasn't going to hurt her. I doubled the amount, and she smiled reluctantly. I promised that later on I'd ring and pay for a taxi to take her home.

As we drove back I explained about losing my wife. I told her I wanted to make a night of it, wanted the comfort of the house, of some decent music, good food and a little bit of conversation before we began. I wasn't afraid of revealing these things to her because it seemed the gentlemanly thing to do considering.

She relaxed, convinced I was some lonely man who'd recently lost his wife and simply needed some female company for one night. She could have said 'why so soon after', or 'couldn't you have gone closer to home', any of the things most people in her business would have asked, but I guess the truth is the money I was paying her was too good to spoilt it by asking questions.

When we arrived at the house she asked if she could see

Rock Hill in it entirety. She told me she was thirty-six and had never seen anything as luxurious and up-market as the house. She called it sinful. Its size startled her, and as I gave her the tour she made sounds at the back of her throat that I took for admiration, stroking the wallpaper, padding across the deep carpets in her bare feet, her eyes gliding over the framed photographs, the furniture, the books, the ornate fixings, the simple restrained elegance of my study, her explorer's curiosity a smile that never strayed far from her rouged lips. Part of me felt proud to see her enjoyment, but I also kept thinking about how she'd stumbled into a predators' lair despite its apparent splendors. Luxurious? Not with Lana paradoxically rotting away in the deep earth, as she convalesced in the freezing waters of the river.

I fixed her a drink while she selected something from the record collection. She didn't choose a CD, but quietly worked her way through Lana's vinyl collection, nimbly picking out the sleeves and turning them over as if the records would shatter unless handled with overstated delicateness. She examined them carefully like a collector would, as if they represented something far more important to her, which I'm certain they did. I suspected there were records in Lana's collection which she recalled from childhood, objects which connected her with some special moment when she was a young girl, before the humiliating realization of why she stood in some ugly nondescript backstreet on an industrial estate every late evening.

When I returned with her red wine, she was sitting on the sofa by the fireplace, flames crawling over the logs spitting at the hearth as if trying to warn her. This woman was somebody's daughter, but seeing her properly for the first time I realized childhood had end prematurely for her that somebody or something had dragged her kicking and screaming into a life already in decline.

We talked for an hour until her eyes closed and her head jerked backwards with sudden and violent force. She was asleep within seconds, one leg curled up beneath her, her tacky red nylon dress hitched at her knees to reveal scarred legs and swollen ankles, her entire history traceable in the very surface of her flesh.

I put my drink down, went into the kitchen and opened the back door. I walked down the garden, the slope speeding my momentum to the fence. When I reached it, I kicked furiously at the wooden slats, the splintered parts spinning away into space before crashing into the river.

I shouted Lana's name, hearing its distant echo tumbling over the water. I pretended it was her replying, telling me she was waiting, that I should hurry. But back in the house I sat and watched the woman sleep. She'd once been very pretty, and I also thought she'd been a cheerful woman, even optimistic at one time.

I got a blanket, covered her with it and before I could change my mind, I went up to bed and left her to sleep.

(26)

In the early hours of the morning the woman came looking for me to apologize. She offered to give me the money back, but I refused, telling her I'd call a taxi and was glad to have had her company regardless.

"It's never happened to me before," she said.

"Spoken like a true bloke," I joked.

She laughed, exposing the terrible decay of her teeth which only made me realize I'd been right in not taking her to Lana. I gave her money for the taxi and something extra for the hours she'd spent asleep on the sofa. She appeared bewildered, even suspicious of my generosity, but I knew she'd have worked the night if I hadn't come along, that she'd have climbed into a half dozen cars to perform undignified acts in an undignified part of town

When she was gone I went up to the study to start a new story. I didn't even think about drinking. The story came out of me as if the woman had reached inside with her hard callused fingers and brought it to the fore.

(27)

By midday I'd written three chapters of a new novel with no foreseeable ending in sight. I liked that. I phoned Colin to tell him and listened to the hesitancy in his voice. I soothed him with believable explanations. "I'm not taking refuge in a fictional reality, don't be so bloody absurd." He made some more noise to protest my career suicide, but he was merely operating under his own perverse guidelines of agency etiquette and finally I put him out of his misery by saying: "Lana would have wanted it." He didn't argue with that. How could he? The ironic thing was I telling the truth.

(28)

The River Place debuted at number one in the paperback charts and sold doubly in the digital market. It had taken me just one month to complete it. Colin made a lot of money from it, and I became what they often call an overnight publishing sensation, as if I hadn't existed previously to the best seller charts noting my arrival. It also opened the door for as many potential victims as I could manage.

The first was an insufferably tedious producer from a minor film company operating out of Manchester. He constantly kept referring to himself as 'a writer at heart' and myself as 'wielding a scalpel of prose,' whatever that was meant to imply. He tried convincing me to sell the rights to The River Place for what was not only a insulting sum for such a successful novel, but was unashamedly offered because he genuinely thought I'd no clue. He must have thought this former darling of the literati had no conception of what constituted fair and what did not. Choosing him was the easiest of all the people who came to stay at Rock Hill. I felt nothing when I tied the rope around his hefty corpse and lowered it through the gap in the fence until his body splayed across the rock. Under cover of darkness, Rock Hill was a perfect location for such things.

I guess it wasn't long after I'd gone back into the house that Lana came for the feast that was Ryan Purfleet, because in the morning nothing remained of the film agent. I like to imagine her as she might have been that first night, entangled in dripping weeds, with silt in her hair and beneath her lengthening fingernails.

(29)

In the summer Jack came home from university. I hadn't seen him since the funeral. I felt I was no more his father than he must have felt that he was my son. I'd betrayed him quite willingly, swapped my duties for that of murderer, denied my only child for the resurrected corpse of his mother in the river. But aren't all families rich with such betrayals? Sometimes they come back singing your praises and sometimes they come wanting your head on a pike. I had Lana, the river and Rock Hill for company. There was no room for any boarders.

(30)

Jack studied all that summer, while I worked on the second book. We were passengers traveling in opposite directions to each other, unheeding of the closeness of our fatal proximities. He went about his studying as if martyred to a cause, his head tilted at an impossible angle so that I was forever having to bend down to see what he was thinking. Not that I cared. I only wanted to make it seem that way.

After a while I gave up altogether. I began leaving yellow post-it-notes stuck to the hallway mirror, little reminders that would read, 'food in the fridge', 'fifty quid on the kitchen table' or 'stop taking my cigarettes – buy your own.' And sometimes I'd find these little scrunched up balls of yellow paper littering the floor, newer ones overlapping the squares of grime that mine had left behind. When the weather turned nasty, with Jack down in his room, and me up in the study writing myself into fictional oblivion, Rock Hill would creak its distress as if we were living inside the hull of a badly deigned boat. I prayed for the whole thing to come crashing down and bury me where I stood, that I might be left there as a testimony to one man's stupidity. But my war of uneasy silence with Jack kept me afloat, the pair of us manning our posts of indignation like soldiers from warring states, permanently fixed on each other for fear the other might sneak a surprise attack. For a father it should have been heartbreaking. For a writer it was heaven sent material.

When his girlfriend from university turned up unannounced, naturally an argument ensued. I told him the house was not large enough to accommodate a third person. He looked at me in disbelief. I invoked Lana's memory and he spat out my name as if it were poison. His girlfriend stood watching us in the hallway, a small beige suitcase in both hands, shock spreading over the soft curves of her face.

"Go fuck yourself," he said as he jumped into his girlfriend's battered Fiat, sticking his head out the passenger window to shout some further obscenity, one more plaintive cry.

I ran after him, waving my arms, a pretense at being the righteous father, but happy I'd chased the pair of them away, relieved Rock Hill was mine once again.

An hour later Lana's parents rang to ask what was happening? I told them to mind their own business. They slammed the phone down. I think Lana's mother called me a 'heartless bastard.' They didn't ring again. Later I thought I saw Lana's face framed in the window of my study, but it was only a reflection of a wish.

(31)

A week after the scene with Jack I received a package in the post. It was from the hospital where Lana had died, inside of which was a mobile phone with a cracked casing. It was Lana's phone. There was a typed letter from an administrator for the return of possessions of former patients.

I switched on the mobile and the battery icon instantly began flashing, but I was luckily able to access the last of her received text messages. Just three words. **Will ring back.** I looked at the date as the screen went blank. It was the same day Lana had slipped off the step into the irretrievable darkness of death. I threw my cigarette into the dried up pile beside the back door and rang her publishers. It took the receptionist a full minute to grasp it was her I wanted to speak to, not Lana's former editor.

I asked whether she'd been working on reception that day. She said she'd been the one who'd called the ambulance, that she'd put her coat over Lana as she lay bleeding and just how terribly sorry she was for my loss. She told me they had a picture of her hanging in the main conference room.

"Was she on the phone when she was leaving?" I asked.

"Yes," came the reply.

(32)

There's blood everywhere. Some of it will be easy to find. Some of it will be invisible, infinitesimal particles splashed into high dusty corners, beneath the cornice, spattered, the hardest to reach parts of the ceiling, evidence of the real evidence. Eventually they will come and this time they will not leave until they have their proof. They will build a forensic world right here in this room, designated zones, science gone mad in its scrupulous intensity. People will stand here and pass judgment, but their analysis will only reveal part of the truth.

(33)

The conversation interested me for once, and I was sad to let the faint connection we shared slip away as the drugs began to work. The fire threw his face into shadow, made him look younger than he was. I was glad I'd given him a heavy dose, it wouldn't take long. I thought Lana should know so I went down to the hole in the fence to tell her. Below the river whispered along the banks, softly twining against the sands, steel grey in the night. I explained everything to her, but if my dead wife was listening she didn't show. I went back into the house and wrapped Jack's body in black bin liners. I put my ear to his chest to make sure, but I could hear nothing. When I'd finished, I lit a cigarette. I'd decided to give him directly to the river, despite him having being responsible for his mother's death. After all, the rock was for strangers. The river was for family.

Not The End Of The Story

Clackety- clack, clackety-clack, clackety-clack, clackety-clack, clackety-clack, clackety-clack, ping.

* * *

Snow drifted off the arc lights towering above the walls of the interrogation center, guards patrolling the battlements and viewing the outside world through dark hooded eyes. Another Corman Grau cliché, once again ridiculing his seldom travelled imagination. Subzero temperatures, too. What next? A charge of hussar cavalry scything through civilians along the boulevards? I moved away under the milky glow of street lights, thinking it it'd been a mistake listening to Mazurek, stamping out the cough in my chest as I entered a milk bar.

Steam rose above the countertop, damp looking food coagulating behind glass hatches, bawdy women in food stained aprons like surgeons in bloody smocks, serving people swaddled and stinking of the capital. I bought a plate of fried pierogi and walked across the room past tables swathed in cigarette smoke. I sat on a high stool in front of the window to get a good view, the plate cupped in one hand, the fork in the other. The interrogation center was a misty blur through the condensation. I tried to picture Grau appearing at the gates, blinking triumphantly through his usual false humility. I couldn't, it didn't seem possible. Once feted, and once the Chancellor's favorite, he was now the fallen figurehead of a vanished intelligentsia. He was an effete literary minstrel, he wouldn't endure but five minutes with the LBK's best interrogators.

I suspected his admirers had gone into hiding, possibly underground, down in the sewers among the street children and rats. I imagined them weakly echoing their revolutionary sentiments through the city's Byzantine plumbing "...our wounded laureate Corman..." the rattling pipes of tenement buildings amplifying their anxieties, afraid even of this audience. At the hour of his martyrdom, it was all a tedious disappointment.

I barely tasted the pierogi, wondering if Grau's death would be any different than the dependable imagery he often described, the bedraggled partisan cowering in the rain in front of a firing squad of young boys, or the *worker* discovered dead in some grimy doorway, an empty bottle of liquor between his splayed legs. Grau could piss enough clichés to burst the banks of the great city.

As I was finishing off the pierogi, an old man who'd been listening to an transistor radio with a half-eaten plate of cutlets to one side, stood up and shouted for quiet. The room fell into a pervasive atmosphere of almost instant solemnity. This was the moment when they'd elevate Grau from death to the role of the unassailable. The revolutionaries, those who'd surely come whether today or fifty years on, would erect to him his own mausoleum. No doubt it'd be a resplendent monstrosity. I pictured foreign tourists having their photographs taken outside of it, thus giving him the fame he'd so stridently denounced while alive.

The old three ringed circus rusting in the wind.

Grau was a second rate novelist to me, one who regularly contradicted the slumbering behemoth that was our government, while secretly courting its patronage for fear of falling sales. I suspected he possessed no moral centre whatsoever. Only the desertion of the intelligentsia had awarded him any kind of credibility.

All eyes were on the old man, as if he were himself a member of the LBK. A woman waiting at the counter for her food, scowled as I delivered my plate through the kitchen hatch.

As I reached the door an astonished gasp went up from the patrons, quickly followed by a huge cheer. I hadn't heard the radio announcer's pronouncement, but the congratulatory faces told me all I needed to know. Anton Mazurek had been right after all. Grau's execution had seemed inevitable, and I doubted the LBK had even stood in the same room as him. I left the milk bar amid a scene of backslapping and impending revelry.

* * *

There were more lights in the windows of the capital's tenements than when I'd entered the milk bar. They'd received news of Grau's impending release with hopes that would soon fade.

I'd spent the best part of the late afternoon hoping for a cortege of soldiers draped in the hypocritical colors afforded state funerals, a twelve gun salute and the scraggly shapes of birds taking to the sky in a startled flurry. Funny how they could denounce you, while at the same time bury your mutilated corpse amidst a warily orchestrated mourning, one dreamt up by the Bureau in deference to the Chancellor's wishes.

With the darkness drawing in, the traffic on the boulevards honking their horns in celebration, some of the drivers leaning out their windows to shout Grau's name, I realized it was time to visit Mazurek to see what he'd planned. I walked down a street of high white walls with barbed wire strung across the tops, embassy buildings with shuttered windows, indistinct figures behind the glass, people in exile. CCTV cameras followed me as I slipped awkwardly between the bumpers of cars, the faces of the drivers returning to their customary truculence now that news of Grau's release added nothing exciting to their lives.

Across from the Bulgarian embassy was Godley Park, beggars emerging in clouds of misted breath like professional greeters. Swans perched on the frosted banks of the ornamental lake, pecking forlornly at the detritus at the water's edge. I turned left along a gravel path following the curve of the pond, sidestepping a gang of children pelting stones at one another, cutting through a crowd of Bulgarian tourists queuing for the fairground rides, even their faces darkened by some unvoiced despondency.

I left the park and entered a street with gas lamps flickering cradles in rows. The government claimed the tourists liked to see such relics, saying it added a halcyon romanticism to the city. People joked that the only thing it gave these back streets was a camouflage better suited to the people who lurked there.

I found the building in a cul-de-sac of derelict warehouses, candles illuminating a hand carved wooden sign behind a dusty window. *The Garret.* I was suddenly conscious of the city settling into its nightly cadences, sounds made obscure by a silky darkness threading between slate rooftops. A characteristic Grau night, theatrically ominous.

I entered the tavern, the cloying heat from an open fire hitting me at once. Several irritated faces glanced in my direction and I quickly closed the door. A large man with an eye-patch stumbled past, loudly cursing in what sounded like Hungarian. Abraham Mendelssohn from Grau's semi-autobiographical 'The King's House.'

The manageress, a woman with chestnut colored hair brushed into artistic swirls across the top of her skull, recognized me and leaned on the pump handle. Hannah Arlene Muller, one of our most celebrated characters, even if 'Astronomer's Delight' had been a critical failure at the time of its publication.

She poured me a beer.

"If you're here, it must be bad, "she said.

Ever since the publication of Master Piquet I'd spent the last twelve years traveling across the country for contracts taken out on people the ordinary citizens were too afraid to do themselves. I often worked under aliases, the names taken from obscure novels by forgotten writers.

"Mazurek was right," I said.

"He always is."

I took the beer and scanned the room. Three elderly women were sitting on foot stools by the fire, their faces like petrified wood in the orange glow of the flames, identical to one another. The Kapolei triplets.

Lloyd Weimar and Gabriella Spencer stood talking in a corner of the room and I couldn't imagine how these turn of the century protagonists from 'Flowers Bequeathed,' could pass unnoticed in clothing which had gone out of fashion during the last Tsar's reign.

I struck a match off the top of the stone hearth, the Kapolei sisters sitting there like victims of Medusa's fatal stare. I lit a cigar stub I'd been saving, puffing on it with mock concentration, while eavesdropping on Weimar and Spencer. I expected to hear the clipped formalities of a language once contained in books long since disposed of. Instead they surprised me with their rather effective idiomatic language, which clashed with their clothing.

Spencer pointed me out.

"He never did get the hang of it," she said.

She must have been referring to the time I spent working as a detective for the Siberian Rail Company before defecting to the Underground. My job had been to seek out conspirators escaped from the gulags, of which there were more than enough despite the Bureau's propagandists denouncing the icy wasteland as holding nothing more than a few moderate work prisons for murderers and cut throats.

"The clothes, right?" Weimar gestured at his brightly colored waistcoat.

"Our identity papers say we're actors," Spencer chimed. Her ball gown resembled a lady's Victorian funeral shroud.

"And they believe you?" I asked, marveling they'd identity papers, not that they were pretending to be actors.

"The Chancellor loves his theatre, there are plenty of us types floating round. We just affect, and the soldiers leave us alone," she replied.

They helped put names to faces, some of which came more readily than others. There was one group I'd absolutely no idea about at all until Weimar told me they were from

Grau's first published work, 'The Bee Keeper Tale,' a collection of short stories written in the avant-garde style of the time.

Their simplicity amused me, the way they waved people over with breezy expressions and cheerful exclamations, unconscious of the stereotypes Grau had landed them with. But they were family and I was happy to see them. The one contribution Grau had made in all of this was inadvertently making us equals. There were none more loyal to the cause of solidarity than us fictional characters.

Which is why Mazurek had finally decided to bring us all together under one roof.

Grau's fiction had been changing the country for some time, we were proof enough of that. But what he'd described in his latest manuscript would be the end of everything. The operatic intensity was too dreadful even for a mercenary like myself. Martyred clergy already hung crucified along some of the back roads.

"We know he keeps the manuscript in a clothes trunk under his bed in Madam Beaufort's," said Weimar.

They told me how Grau had started to outline chapters in which among many horrors, he had reduced the populace to a penury worse than any which had come before.

"The country will become rife with the stench of rot and decay," Spencer said, closing a delicate hand over her freckled bosom. "That's what he wrote."

"In one chapter he has exploded trains choking rail-lines, the wrecks of cars littering the streets," Weimar added. "He actually described it as 'like the forgotten memories of passing strangers.' What on earth could that mean?"

Spencer tugged at my sleeve as Mazurek appeared in the doorway. He'd dressed in a military uniform, medals fastened to the lapels of a handsome black jacket, a red cap with a grey band circling the peak clasped under one arm and a pair of black trousers which appeared carved from stone such was their crispness. Lastly a ceremonial sword hung across his broad chest in a jeweled sheath. His wide nostrils flared once for dramatic effect.

"My God," Weimar declared, "he's come as himself."

"What does he look like?" Spencer giggled.

I gave them a quick glance.

"Ah, but that's different," Spencer blushed, "actors remember. And him?" She jerked an accusing finger in his direction.

She had a point, for there was nothing in Mazurek's back story that even hinted at a military past.

Muller brought out an empty wine chest for Mazurek to stand on and as he did he calmly swept his officious gaze over the room. Every face turned to him, some expectantly, some more nervously. Outside the tavern a horse clomped past the window, an inconsistency with the present, another portent of what was coming.

Mazurek spoke.

"It was the Chancellor who once decreed God a moot point here in this secular wasteland of ours, before the church dug its claws back in. Ironic, eh, considering the chancellor's friendship with Corman Grau, our ignoble creator. And as for the LBK..." he laughed, "...they'd no more harm the Chancellor's pet than repeal their medieval laws."

"And what shall we do?" somebody yelled.

Many of the people in the room, grousing better than their ordinary counterparts ever could have, grumbled their agreement.

"Do you propose we kill him?" Irena Lovett asked.

The voices died down, everybody turning their attention to the tiny figure lying on a couch near the window with the sign, her useless legs raised on silk pillows. Lovett was a crippled ballerina, a bromide of our country's literature. Grau hadn't needed an imagination when writing her, he'd stolen her from any number of dated classics.

"I do," said Mazurek.

Again, whispered dissent.

Mazurek raised his arms cruciform as if impelling us to challenge his Christ like pose.

"Will you be my volunteers? " he asked.

Spencer looked at me, mouthing the word, *my*.

"For what?" shouted Angus Crux, who'd been a traveling circus strongman in Grau's twelfth novel, The Drowning Of A Soldier. His bald head looked like a granite slab on shoulders shaped like parapets.

"For a suicide squad," I said.

"The insurrection, or whatever you want to call it, will be exactly that," Muller said, folding an apron over the counter.

"Will there be casualties? I cannot say," Mazurek whispered back at us.

"You mean you won't say," said Weimar, no longer so cheerful looking.

Mazurek sighed as if we were a class of idiots, and he'd been sent to educate us out of our ignorance.

"Look at us all, gathered in force like the good folk Grau never intended us for. And...," he said, stabbing the air at several faces closest to him, "you came freely, willingly."

There was a small cheer from the crowd reminiscent of the people in the milk bar at the announcement of Grau's release.

Mazurek beamed, encouraged.

"Why should we care? Indeed, why should we give the slightest notion to these ordinary folk? We've no connections to these people, we've no responsibility to them at all. Look at this wretched country. Has it not resembled a fever dream for too long? Why should we intervene with what Grau now intends."

He paused.

"But that *is* exactly what Corman Grau would have us do. *Nothing*. This man, this so called writer of the people," Mazurek flapped his hand as if Grau was standing right in front of him and spat on the floor, "would expect nothing less than our total obedience, that we should bear witness to this, the greatest of all his entertainments. Be warned. He will surely welcome this approaching catastrophe as if it were a missive from the Lord Christ himself." As he turned on the wine chest his brilliantly polished boots squeaked. A skewed shaft of street light came through the window. "Do you really think he'd listen to us? Us? In his eyes we are unfaithful and abnormalities, betrayers of our creator. Given the chance he will not hesitate to snuff us out and start over again."

Mazurek, having finally captivated his audience continued to give an oratory symphonic in its construction a superfluity of words transfixing us, even if against our better judgment. It was indeed the end of everything.

* * *

The next evening I crouched under the back kitchen window to a boarding house not far from Capital Square. From my position I could see if somebody were to come up the path but the house had only two occupants, neither of whom were expecting any visitors except for the shift change of the bodyguards assigned to watch over Grau. The next changeover was at midnight. The corpses of the present shift lay several feet away, their faces devoid of expression.

I waited until ten o'clock and was about to check my watch to be sure, when there was the sound of gunfire coming from the direction of Capital Square. I emerged, glancing up the street as the gunfire grew more rapid. I walked round to a side door and rapped with as much authority as I could.

Somebody coughed on the other side and a bolt drew back, the door opening a fraction. I kicked it inwards before it could shut on me. It hit the woman on the other side and wedged her against the hallway wall, her eyes glassy with terror.

"Which room is Grau's?" I asked.

She blanched at hearing his name and despite the weight of the revolver I'd pulled from my coat pocket and pressed into her throat, she crossed her self and muttered a prayer. Blood flowed from her nose where the door had hit her. I squeezed my finger round the trigger of the revolver Mazurek had given me the night before.

"I won't even waste a bullet on you, I'll stamp your head into the carpet instead, understand?" I thrust the revolver into the sagging flesh beneath her chin.

She lifted a shaking hand to the stairs ahead of us.

"Door at the end of the corridor. It's the only upstairs room on that side of the house."

* * *

"A life was lost in acquiring this information," Mazurek said the evening before as we sat in the Garret discussing his

43

plans. "Without Stanley Neville, I don't think we'd ever have found out about this bolt hole of Grau's."

I knew Neville was a self-exiled Englishman from the novel, Liars Leap, who'd a skill for squeezing information out of the most reluctant of sources, many of whom just happened to be female.

"The LBK officer, the one whose wife he slept with, that's what happened. He got sloppy. Nevertheless, he was a good man."

A good man? The way he said it I thought he no more regarded Neville's death than he did a stray dog run over in the street. There was a moment's silence as Mazurek pretended to honor Neville, before he continued.

"If anybody's suited to this, then you're definitely it."

"One man? That's hardly a ruse," I protested.

"But we're the distraction."

"Everybody?"

The room, empty of people (Mazurek had dismissed them as he would have men in the army), except for Muller, who was busy moping the bare stone flags around the hearth, had the same unnatural quietness as Mazurek's eyes were showing.

"Not all of us."

"Naturally," I scoffed.

"Look, when the ordinary populace get wind of what we've done, it'll mean no more living on the fringes, no more scuttling about like infants with shit in our pants."

"But one man?"

"There'll be only two agents, babysitters. No trouble at all."

"How do you know the Chancellor won't make a scene of his benevolence, and release Grau out the front gate?"

"Because Grau was never there."

"What?"

"The LBK never arrested him."

"But why?"

"Good question. Maybe it's some sort of twisted publicity stunt."

"For Grau's masterpiece?"

"Who knows. It's as much a mystery to the LBK, as it is to us. The assault on the interrogation center is a smokescreen, but we want them to know we want Corman Grau dead. It might seem bizarre to them at first, but once word gets out, once they know, they'll come flocking."

It was pitch black outside, even the street lamps making little impression on the night.

"And you're sure we can't get to the manuscript?" I pressed.

"And what if we could? It wouldn't do us any good. And who's to say he won't improve on the last draft. Besides, we'd never get past Madam Beaufort's lobby, let alone to Grau's floor. So what does it matter why the Chancellor denounced Grau."

"It matters a great deal since I've two LBK officers to dispose of. You realize the Chancellor will have handpicked these men himself."

But Mazurek wasn't exaggerating the hotel's impregnability. We knew that of the six rooms on the top floor, the LBK occupied all but Grau's executive suite. We had a better chance of storming the interrogation center.

From Neville we'd learned that the Chancellor had secretly arranged for Grau to escape to a boarding house whenever Madam Beaufort's hotel became too much of a nuisance for him to write. I, on the other hand, suspected this was merely Grau playing the part of the reclusive genius driven mad by supposed distractions.

"You'll trap him in a cheap room in a cheap boarding house and dispatch him to the one place even his writing can't save him from," Mazurek said.

"Do you really believe the ordinary people will thank us for this?"

"Only an idiot would deny the suddenness of these changes that Grau committed against his own."

"And the Chancellor?"

"One step at a time."

In the first year of my existence I met a priest travelling east along the same countryside roads as I was heading west in search of employment. I told him my identity as he took my confession on the floor of a dilapidated barn in the middle of summer, and I remember the hayloft awash with flies buzzing over the corpse of a dead cat.

The priest described me as God's surety, his magnificent kindness.

"Be rested and safe in this," he'd said.

These days when I think of the priest I think of Grau. Mazurek could be wrong, our accidental creator might think us miracles, and might even abandon his present manuscript.

Mazurek stood up and placed a revolver on the table between us.

"Muller will tell you the rest." He held out his hand and we shook.

"Not you then?"

"Our people are waiting," he replied as if we were complicit in his leadership, "good luck."

He left the way he'd come, only this time there was no one to watch him go.

* * *

I used a length of parcel twine that I kept in my pockets at all times (easier than carrying round a foot length of rope) to bind the landlady's legs and arms to a broken radiator in the hallway. When she started to talk I tapped the butt of the revolver against her forehead. It didn't stop her, so I tore the hem from her apron and stuffed it into her mouth. She shook her head, staring at me knowingly.

"Heard it all before, babushka." I turned out the light and mounted the stairs to Grau's room.

When I reached the landing I listened for Grau moving about in his room. There were lamps set about on tiny wooden trestle tables and I could hear the fizz of their faulty wiring, but otherwise the house was quiet.

There was a single door was at the end of the corridor as the landlady had described. There was a washbasin on the floor near my feet and as I crept past I made sure not to kick it. I put my ear to Grau's door, but I could only hear the traffic coming through an open window somewhere in the house.

Flushed with nerves, my elbow tucked in against my ribcage like a halted piston, I aimed the revolver at the door, shakily reaching for the door knob, a single bead of sweat rolling down the side of my face like something out of a Grau novel.

Just before I had my hand on the door knob I heard the metallic clang of the washbasin as somebody walked into it. I turned and fired the revolver once, hitting the landlady in the throat, more by accident than by design. There was a spray of arterial blood and both of the landlady's hands lapped uselessly at the hole where her throat had been,

47

giving me a look that instantly penetrated my panic. How had she escaped? She spun round, making a dry retching sound, pivoted sideways and fell over the top step and down the stairs.

I threw the door wide open, waving my gun ahead of me.

The room had a single occupant who was clearly not Grau, a man so enormous he dwarfed the writing desk at which he was sitting, and while his face looked familiar to me, I failed to register who he was.

He smiled at the shakily held revolver pointed straight at him and I vaguely wondered why he wasn't already on his feet. Sensing my bewilderment he slowly got to his feet, his bulk swaying. He was even taller than I'd thought, his head scraping against the ceiling.

"You must be Corman's assassin," he boomed, his voice shaking the porcelain plates standing on a mantle-piece. His head moved on a neck I couldn't see for the rolls of flesh billowing there, his small black eyes like grease spots.

"Where's Grau?" I asked.

He made no attempt to come at me, but instead inched open the high starched collars of his black suit jacket. There was a crown of black hair circling the top of his skull and a brown birth mark on his right cheek. He puffed out his chest, and instantly grew another five or six inches in every direction. His head inclined down from the limitations of the ceiling.

"Where is he?" I repeated, raising the revolver.

With his back to the room's only window, most of the street light trickled round his shoulders with a flickering intensity. He looked devilish.

"Are you frightened?" he asked.

I'd garroted, axed, strangled and drowned dozens of lunatics over the years. I knew I could move faster than he could, that he wouldn't have anywhere near the skill to match my speed. The bigger they are, the harder they fall, right? Yet I couldn't help but imagine myself stood under him if he fell.

"I want Grau," I said.

He laughed, another inch added to his frame.

"Corman is nowhere at all," an earthquake sound in his throat, "and that friend of yours, Mazurek, he also is nowhere at all. Like all of your friends...all gone, all gone....all except you."

It came to me.

"I recognize you," I said.

"And what?"

I showed him.

I fired six times in quick succession, the bullets making a soft whap, whap sound as they struck him. His jacket, straining on his gargantuan frame, puffed out at the impact of the shots, but the white shirt beneath failed to darken with the spread of blood.

"Oooooh," he said.

I fired again, but the revolver clicked on an empty chamber.

He stood there unhurt, still expanding, staring down at me with a quizzical bemusement. He glanced at his stomach, inserting the tip of a finger in the smoking circle just above his navel.

"Is that it?" he asked.

I dropped the revolver to the floor, turned and ran out of the room. I rounded the top of the stairs as he gave out a victorious harrumph, this monstrous man painfully squeezing himself through the doorway like a rat out of a drainage pipe, something bloated and huge. I went down the stairs on my back like a kid sledging in winter. I flew off the bottom step, skidding along the floor of the hallway, the corpse of the landlady halting my escape.

The corpse sat up, smiling.

"Plenty of vacancies," she said.

The corners of her mouth constricted, opening the wound in the throat even wider, a second mouth gaping. I screamed. The landlady, mimicking my distress, screamed also, but the sound came not from her mouth but from the hole below her chin. A jagged splinter tore through the ceiling, plaster dust raining onto the landlady's corpse face. She grinned, spitting a tooth in my direction. "Keep it if you like," the flatness of her voice somehow made it worse. She fell onto her hands and knees, scuttling towards me on all fours like a demented gymnast. "Here I come."

There was a shuddering roar as a human fist the size and width of a mechanical shovel punched straight through the ceiling. I scrambled out of the way as a large chunk of masonry crashed down behind me, wedging itself tight against the front door, preventing my escape. Very slowly the gigantic fist turned on the end of that long hairy arm, opening like a colossal umbrella and stretched it fingers. Its knuckles cracked, sounding like construction beams slotting into place. A pool of blood, dark and viscous, pattered onto the floor from the giant's wrist, a flap of skin hanging wetly from the shattered edges of the hole it'd created in the ceiling. The hand turned again, like some predator trying to locate its prey.

The landlady lay on her side like a stunned insect. Above us both a huge glaring eye stared down, blinking away plaster dust. The hand reached out and picked up the landlady, its grotesquely sized fingers pinning her within the ample circumference of its vast palm. Its thumb casually stroked her head as if playing with a doll, before the hand snapped shut. The landlady's skull popped as if it were a grape, her brains exuding from between those enormous fingers. The giant gave a simple flick of its wrist, discarding the landlady's corpse which sailed limply through the air, splattering against the wall in an explosion of gore and viscera.

I wanted to put my hands over my eyes, pretend the mangled remains of the corpse weren't oozing down the wallpaper, but when the giant's hand started moving in my direction, walking its fingers across the hallway floor, I opened my mouth instead and began to scream.

* * *

It felt ~~like~~ as if it were still winter, my breath a shapeless mass, a distillation of my growing impatience. Ice crystals were already forming on the pavements like scattered gem stones. The cold sank through the layers of clothing in search of precious body heat. They said the temperature was a bitter anomaly, but others were claiming it was impossible for this time of year.

The day before I'd heard one old man say to his wife on the back seats of a packed tram that he thought the cold was symbolic.

"Symbolic of what?" his wife asked.

"Something dark and terrible has descended," he continued.

"But symbolic of what?"

The old man saw me watching and told his wife to be

51

quiet. In a country like ours this was a common sight. We intimated the unspeakable, an encoded language, conversing without speaking.

But the old man, despite stinking of alcohol, was right in a way, something dark and terrible *had* descended.

Corman Grau.

I continued to watch the guards, bat like shapes moving under the arc spotlights along the walls of the interrogation center. I counted how many there were, anything that helped pass the time. The cold made me feel as if I'd been standing there all day, or at least some other day, one I couldn't remember. I shook the sensation off and stared at that unremarkable building, as if my belligerence alone could force Grau outside.

Something told me the LBK would soon release him, but why I'd ever think such a thing I couldn't say. Had somebody already warned me? *Once feted, the Chancellor's favorite, he was the literary figurehead of a disappeared intelligentsia.* There it was again, a line from something I'd read. It had happened to me yesterday. It was about Grau, but where had I heard it?

I needed to eat something and so I crossed Capital Square to a milk bar I'd seen on my way over. Before I could open the door something caught my eye. A shape moved behind the clouds, reflecting off the moon.

At the hour of his martyrdom, it was all a tedious disappointment. Another one of those lines, and once more something shifted beyond the clouds. I heard low guttural laughter. At the same time something inconceivably tall moved along the city skyline.

What was that?

To the northeast was the Arcadia, one of the city's mos

famous hotels. Mounted on its roof behind fifteen foot high letters spelling out its name was a spotlight which often swept the sky in the evenings to advertise its whereabouts. Maybe I was simply seeing some sort of optical effect.

I changed my mind about the milk bar and decided I was no longer so hungry. It felt wrong not entering, somehow an inconsistency in my character. It was as if I'd disobeyed some natural expediency of events. And it occurred to me I'd absolutely no idea what I was going to do next.

I let my feet decide.

I walked as if along a predetermined route, one which somebody had laid out for me like train tracks. There was no conscious decision making involved, moving across the city without really seeing it. Soon I was passing under the rusting iron work sign for Godley Park, having very little memory of walking twenty city blocks in less than thirty minutes.

The swans were gone. (What swans?) No matter how hard I looked I wouldn't find them. For some reason *he'd* changed his mind about including them. Not only that, but the tourists standing in line for the fairground rides were speaking in French, not Bulgarian.

I could hear somebody at a typewriter. The hairs on my arms stood on end.

I looked around, convinced there must be an open window somewhere, that the sound was carrying. But as well as there being no buildings for half a mile, there were too many tourists (they should be Bulgarian), too many people in general for me to be able to hear something so clearly distinctive.

I heard laughter again, the typewriter carriage shunting back and forth like a loom in a textile factory

...the beggars emerging in clouds of misted breath...

But there were no beggars or swans, only foreigners speaking in French. The noise of the typewriter rocked the trees. The park lights intensified, bright explosions within their glass cases, illuminating the subtlety of the changes.

Go to him.

The thought, whether really mine or put there, was unavoidable.

I followed the sound of the typewriter as the children of Hamelin had once followed the man with the pipe. I passed people I knew were lesser kinds of fiction than myself. The trees swayed in musical undulations, their branches rubbing together excitedly. The park lights flickered, announcing my approach, corridors appearing, intersecting with the paths. A pair of eyes stared down at me through the branches of a tree. I covered my face until they were gone.

This is not the end.

Some of the foliage had outgrown its borders and burst through the neat topiary of the hedgerows, spreading across the paths, a green flood entangling my feet. The temperature dropped, my *breath a shapeless mass in front of my face, a distillation of my patience.*

Had they been *his* words from the very start?

The typewriter stopped.

The lamps in the park were electric, not gas, but they made strange wavering patterns on the ground which crunched underfoot, a crackling sheen of ice stretching out before me, a glacial plain swimming in mist. Somewhere I'd left the path and wandered out onto the frozen surface of a lake. Only there was no lake in Godley Park, only a pond. Just as the tourists visiting the fairground were meant to be Bulgarian, not French.

No swans.

There was a house standing on the lake, a shimmering ice-cake structure with rows of serried stalagmites circling it. The mist floated round the house, but did not obscure it. It was a long walk out there, and I was afraid the ice would break, but before I could contemplate turning back I was standing on the doorstep.

Hanging from a length of chain above the door was a block of transparent ice, in which sat Anton Mazurek's head. The encased human features were appallingly magnetic and I felt I should smash the block and free the head. Such grim thoughts, but not inexplicable, not now I knew.

I realized the exterior of the house remained a descriptive blank to me except for the block of ice with Mazurek's head. I tried to focus, but the details kept changing, slipping away. A first draft, I thought, that's what this is.

I opened the door and had to shield my eyes from the glaring white brightness within. For some reason I'd imagined the faceless house to comprise of many rooms, but like its outer surface it too remained an unfinished blankness. There was only the light, which darkened noticeably as I lowered my hands.

The Chancellor was sitting at a plain wooden desk, his arms encompassing a huge black antique typewriter.

"Beautiful, isn't she," he said, the typewriter gleaming threateningly. It gave off invisible energy, radiating powerful waves. The Chancellor accidentally hit a key, a shining metallic arm curved like a piece of whalebone catching the brightness in the room as it rose and came back down again, imprinting a letter into the single sheet of paper rolled into the carriage. From this distance I couldn't see how much the

Chancellor had written, but I suspected it wouldn't be much. An enormous manuscript covered in cobwebs lay stacked on the floor by his feet.

"Is it that?" I asked.

He nodded.

The Chancellor, a thin man with a noticeable paunch, lacked any distinguishing features except for the birthmark on his right cheek, hard to imagine this man was the ruler of a country.

"How long have you been playing at Grau?" I asked.

He ran a hand through his thinning black hair, sighing.

"I don't remember."

"Do you intend to finish the book?"

"I do, but it seems to be taking a little longer than I planned."

"Writer's block?"

"I'm afraid it's much worse than that."

"How?"

"This machine, Grau's invention, it made you, gave you a history, a back story, you have some degree of autonomy."

"Until you started altering everything."

"If I hadn't, you and your kind would have run amok long before now."

"Nobody knows we even exist."

"That's simply not the case. The people suspect something is wrong. The old man you heard talking on the tram. The cold was symbolic? Remember?"

"But you wrote that."

"No, *it* did," he said, passing a hand over its primitive casing, admiring it. "Because of you and the others it changes things, usually at random."

"Is Grau dead?"

"Yes, erased."

"The machine or you?"

"Both."

"You decided to rewrite things differently."

"But I didn't write any of what's coming."

"Then abandon the book."

"The machine won't let me."

I closed the door as he continued to speak.

"Have you never noticed how vague everything seems these days, how the present and past mix in some hodgepodge of briefly sketched detail, how the names of the people seem randomly unrepresentative of the country we live in," he said.

"Yes, but..."

"And what country is this?" he broke off, looking down at the typewriter. "Where are we?"

"You must rewrite the story."

Out the corner of my eye changes were occurring.

"I'm lost inside a story," he whispered.

"I can help you get out."

I crossed the room without him seeing.

"Remember the boarding house, that monstrous caricature if made of me, you think it won't do the same to you?"

I'd no idea what he was talking about.

"I could help you finish the book."

"It can't be finished," he said.

I was near enough to smell the sweat on his skin, the Chancellor emitting fear the way the typewriter exuded its power. On his desk was a blue fountain pen, the gold nib uncapped. I'd no memory of it being there before, but as the Chancellor reached for the machine, I snatched it. He inclined his head to see what I was doing, and I rammed the tip into his left ear. There was a moist sucking sound and his eyes rolled up to their whites, his left arm jerking out as if he wanted to embrace me, quietly falling over his desk, covering the typewriter with his body. I waited for him to stop convulsing, before pushing him off.

More of the house swam into focus, a balustrade appearing, a winding staircase, a side room with a white vase with yellow roses on a table in the center of the room. I sat down at the desk and looked at the sheet of paper in the typewriter. It was blank. I'd decided to write what the Chancellor had not. I would write a better history for my country. I would invent where he'd failed to imagine. I would explode the old myths.

I placed my fingers on the keys. I paused, listening for what had sounded to me like another typewriter somewhere, but there was only the creaking of timber as the house grew and expanded and came to life.

Clickety-clack, clickety-clack, clickety-clack, clickety-clack.

AMBIGUOUS

(1)

My grandmother gave me the letter on a cold dreary day which made the hospice darker than ever before, rain striking the half dozen skylights above the long twisting corridors and that faint medicinal smell in the air, a gloomy composite of every depressing thought imaginable.

"When you think you understand what I've written there, you may ask me any questions you like," she said. Her arms were stretched thin within the loose gown she wore, but she raised a hand long enough to touch my cheek. "It's not pleasant, but it's the truth."

I never did get the chance to ask her what that letter meant, what she'd wanted me to understand, whether there was something subtly encoded within the contents or not, something I hadn't recognized on account of my age, or simple inability to grasp, for she died within the hour of me leaving her.

This is what she wrote:

Our ancestry meant the family had a certain amount of standing in circles afar of Chapel Hill, and we often received invitations courtesy of families whose money had long since disappeared into the crass architectural eyesores they inhabited. Thomas often said they were the ghosts of their own convoluted family trees, which made my mother laugh, and left my father irate for hours on end.

Ah, Thomas, I travelled all over the continent with him at a time when women of my background and age seldom moved outside the borders of their closely guarded upbringing. For a while my travels made me a cause célèbre in Chapel Hill, so much so that Thomas described it as an enviable popularity more analogous to an unshakeable infamy. You have to understand that it was a time when gossip mattered in such small communities, when talk between the neighbors had the potency to force people out and ruin reputations. It was a valuable social commodity traded among the villagers as if an illegal, but somehow profitable currency. Nobody quite understood why at twenty years of age I kept disappearing with my elder brother every few months.

Thomas had a successful antique business which accommodated his long-distance affairs with several foreign women, which naturally transpired as a result of the dusty relics he helped tracked down for these wealthy clients of his. I never liked any of these woman, but what cities he took me to see, Bayeux, Madrid, Istanbul. I'd rather ignorantly thought he took me along to bear witness to his notoriety, that I would repeat what I saw to my parents, but I was much too naive to see he was abroad for far more serious reasons.

The replacements, George. They're everywhere. Closer than you think.

That was it, an enigmatic, unsigned ending to an unaddressed grandson, whose sloping letters on that single sheet of paper didn't resemble my late grandmother's handing writing, but looked nearer to the scruffy loose schoolboy writing I employed infrequently, but was instantly recognizable as mine. If I hadn't known better, I might have suspected I'd written it myself.

(2)

The training course took place over four weekends in a nondescript building on the outskirts of the city. I expected it to consist of university graduates, gap year students, people younger than myself, but there were as many middle-aged people seeking foreign lands in the hope of kick-starting their lives back on track as anybody else. Mostly they were easy enough to get along with, but there were one or two so desperate to unload their life stories to anybody within earshot, that it soon became clear TEFL teaching was an escape route for many of them. There was also another contingent, a third group, what I mentally referred to as the incorrigibles. They were ruddy faced and usually heavy smokers, people who unconsciously inhabited a world of brash, theatrical mannerisms and whose voices boomed out like exploding shells of drama in the moderately sized classrooms we worked in. These were the extroverts, the renowned escapees of their own lives, borderline alcoholics.

Every Sunday once the workshops finished, Anita, our instructor, would conclude lessons by inviting everybody over to the Roundhouse pub across the street from the former primary school where we did our training, where those failed actors and therapists, or whatever else it was they claimed to have tried at some time in their lives, displayed a feverish propensity in drinking the rest of us under the table.

I guess I was far too judgmental by half, for I would sit at the end of the table and silently sift through their stories like a detective in pursuit of contradictions, searching out inconsistencies in their fiction, mentally noting the implausibility of what they so often claimed, and even sometimes fantasizing about poking holes in their exaggerated biographies. I enjoyed listening to them if only to share the unspoken acknowledgement of the others, that we knew they were embellishing, if not inventing. But oddly enough these unlikely truths possessed a genuine creativity, a certain flair and secretly I became convinced they'd make great teachers, undoubtedly become the stars of their chosen schools, greatly valued even. But sitting there every week for the duration of the course I began noticing the pub's other regulars elbowing one another over their rolled-up cigarettes, stifling their laughter with endless rounds and whisky chasers. I told myself I understood those men, that coming here each Sunday evening they had to listen to people fabricate and fictionalize their lives so flagrantly, so publicly, that it was impossible not listening in. But nothing could excuse those expressions, or condone the barely suppressed cruelty of their comments, which they'd often make whenever one of us went over to the bar to order a drink.

I'm ashamed to say I wanted to walk over and explain myself, that I wanted to say I was one of them, or if not like them, at least wry enough to recognize outright falsehoods. But that would have been much worse than telling a few stories to a bunch of people we'd probably never see again. Not that I felt any better each time I walked into the pub to see the same people sitting on the same bar stools, who would turn to listen to us as if deigning us worthy of their muffled innuendos.

MOUNTAINS OF SMOKE

At the end of the four weeks I was lucky enough to get a job in Spain. There was no ex-girlfriend propelling me elsewhere, and no other worries at work apart from the tedium of my office job selling gas and water filters for cars. There was only a presumption I was meant to do something else, and whatever that something might have been remains as much a mystery to me now as it did then.

(3)

Two weeks into my stay in Gijon I recall walking along the beach on a weekday evening in early May, feeling contemptuous of the tourists lounging near the shoreline, thinking of myself as more than just another expatriate. Teenagers were playing acoustic guitars on the beach, couples were tossing sticks for their dogs, and elderly people were stroking the water's edge with their bare feet. Each night I'd sit on the veranda of my rented flat near to the school were I worked, and stare out at the ocean with all those boats. I would breathe in the air and say to myself that this was something entirely different. I was grateful for the romance Gijon had ignited within myself, even if it did belong to a commercial stuck between CNN news bulletins. It mightn't have seemed much to the people back home, but for me it was a lot to comprehend. Just thinking about it became a full time preoccupation.

A month into my contract I was sitting on the deck of a yacht that belonged to the father of one of my students, three or four miles off the coast of Gijon, when we came upon the upturned hull of a smaller vessel drifting towards us. Clinging to the hull, seemingly trying to steer the impossible weight of the boat, were two men in lifejackets the color of oranges. The others got them onboard and we

63

radioed the lifeguard before heading back to the harbor. The two men were unharmed, but the lifeboat crew recovered the body of their friend five hours later.

The next day I watched the local news but there was nothing about the accident. The morning I'd climbed onboard the yacht I'd still been a fresh-faced recruit in my own life. Now I might as well have been back home.

I had lessons the following day, but Laura, whose father's yacht it'd been, failed to appear. When she didn't show up the next week either, it was clear she wouldn't return. It was unclear to me whether I felt relief or disappointment as I'd never expected the people in Gijon to resemble those back home. The naivety in thinking this way made me uneasy, and the realization that there were still links between Chapel Hill and myself, that they were imperceptible and so impossible to disentangle from, was impossible to ignore.

I started touring the city's bars after school, waking up in women's apartments in a part of the city that were as familiar to me as the lack of hangovers were becoming. Whenever I climbed out of their beds none of these woman woke or even stirred, their faces pressed so deeply into their pillows as if they were unconsciously trying to suffocate themselves. As I dressed and left the only sound would be their faint breathing. As for their names they remained unknown, invariably relegated to one more in a long line of continuing disappointments.

Towards the middle of June, which is usually the end of the private language school season across the continent, I replied to an advertisement from a school in Warsaw. They were looking for people to teach intensive courses during the summer, with an option for further employment starting in

MOUNTAINS OF SMOKE

September. The woman who conducted the interview over SKYPE spoke with an accent I secretly thought preposterous, invoking images of cold war spies swapping secrets in rundown bars and driving dilapidated Soviet Maluch's across heavily patrolled bridges spanning political ideologies as well as their countries.

The interview went unexpectedly better than I'd anticipated given my issues with using such technology, yet throughout the interview I kept thinking we weren't talking over a distance comprised of thousands of miles, but of insoluble decades that hung in the air between us like asteroid fragments spinning through deepest space. Geography had no part of it, for I became certain I was staring into the face of a woman speaking through time.

At the end of the interview her attitude softened a little, and she asked why I'd applied to a school in Poland as it wasn't often the first choice for native speakers.

"My TEFL instructor taught in Krakow, she said I'd like the people."

This was partially true, but not the real reason for choosing Poland. My mother and father had gone skiing in the Tatra mountains shortly after the dismantling of the Berlin Wall. On their return they'd described the poor facilities, the local people who willfully overran the ski-lifts as if blinded by the snow, the shabby, ruined buildings in whose doorways forbidding characters hovered restlessly, who my father claimed were waiting for somebody to better illustrate the end of Communism and what they were about to inherit. That'd been twenty years ago and much would have changed in all that time, but the imagery had always stuck in my head.

I received an email two days later informing me my

interview had been successful. I wrote back saying I'd come a week earlier so as to fully orient myself with the city.

On the evening before I was due to leave I hired a bicycle and rode along the seafront watching the distant specks of boats on the horizon moving towards one another slowly, like tentative guests at a party. Small puffs of clouds layered the brilliant transparency of the sea, and I wondered if I'd made a mistake accepting the job. Later that night I had a nightmare in which the drowned sailor came to my bedroom window, crying in garbled Spanish we'd left him behind. When I woke I knew I couldn't stay, and as if to support my excuse, the moon appeared through the half drawn blinds, exposing the corners of my room as filled with skulking presences.

(4)

I landed in Warsaw and discerned very few differences between the various nationalities. As far as I could see any of us could have originated from the same country. Even two teenage girls holding hands in arrivals passed by relatively unnoticed. Once I left the airport following Anna's instructions I took a taxi, which naturally, though the driver spoke very little English and overcharged me, allowed me to see some of the city.

Warsaw proved contrary to my hopes. In many ways I could see it was a city still feeling its way through its past, all those wide open spaces between its buildings demonstrative far too much sky for a true urbanite. But there was also a cosmopolitan sheen to the city, its streets swarming with fashionably dressed people enjoying a climate I'd have expected of a Mediterranean country. It was as if I'd got of the plane in the wrong country. There were some reminder of the city's past masters, none more prominent that the Palace of Culture and Science, seven hundred feet of old Soviet dementia poured into a building which subjugated the city skyline to its presence, which some of the older residents had nicknamed Stalin's Syringe. But the construction of new buildings, sleek structures with coruscating bodies and glass topped pinnacles, said people expected more of their capital, which made me arrival all the more confusing.

Everywhere I walked expensive cars filled the streets, and business people moved in cliques of self-importance, shouting into their phones in a language which made Spanish sound feeble, even dispassionate. I only had to see the students in their disparate fashions to feel equally bewildered by my destination.

When I met Anna the confusion intensified. I'd expected a pale-faced, reflective woman, but instead found a beautiful waif with a smart face that belied her sharp tongue. She looked nothing like the woman from our interview over the internet.

She introduced the Polish teachers who exuded a seriousness that was at times overpowering, but once the teaching day ended they reverted back to their social selves. I'd liked the negligent organization of the Spanish, their easy friendliness, but I found myself gravitating to the Polish with far more interest. The questions they asked I expected, but once we were sitting in a bar or chatting away I felt an automatic attraction to their slowly fermenting personalities. I admired them from the offset, curiously aghast at their committed work ethic, likening it more to my mother's generation than my own, their education, their talent for languages, their knowledge of the world, its geography, its countries.

That was not to say there weren't aspect I'd rather have done without. School, for instance, was a military academy of carefully planned hierarchies, where we the subordinates ran round in muffled reverence of our responsibilities. Secretly I loved the nervousness of it all, the rank and file strata of seniority, corrupted in its own Kafkaesque administrative language.

A week into the job two of my advanced students, Slywia and Artur, invited me to spend the weekend with them at a cabin outside of the city. They drove me down in a gleaming Mercedes, delightedly smashing the stereotypes I'd come armed with. By the time we reached the cabin, they'd given me a crash course in Central European politics, Polish history and scientific achievements.

"Marie Curie was Polish?"

The cabin was a cottage among five other expensive looking properties in a fenced off plot of land beside a large lake.

"This is great," I said.

"It is basic," said Artur, "but it is cheap."

"Contract your pronouns and verbs," I said.

"Do people really speak like that in Britain?"

While the others were unloading the car I walked through the trees bordering our side of the property and along a path to the lake. I didn't get very far before I realized somebody was watching me. Fifty feet away near the edge of the lake stood a group of about five or six people whose heads collectively turned in my direction, an action that seemed at once both mechanical and eerily precise.

I only knew one or two Polish words, but I did my best and shouted out so they could hear me: "Dzien dobra." There was no reaction, but they continued to stare at me.

turned around hastily and went back to the cottage.

That weekend we canoed across the lake and visited the crumbling ruins of a castle overlooking the nearby resort of Lagow. I liked Slywia and Artur, but something about them put me off wanting to arrange any future get-togethers. They were too nice, too orderly, too organized.

Graham was the only other native speaker in the school. He was from North Wales, but his accent had vanished, which he said had happened two years into the job.

"How long have you been here?"

"Ten years," he replied. He was in his late forties, and I later found out he had such an intimate working knowledge of the best pubs in town he could have got a job as a tour guide.

The next week I went with him to an Irish pub round the corner from the Tomb of the Unknown soldier. The people inside dressed in Warszawa Legia football tops, drinking amid a cloud of pungent cigarette smoke and hysterical laughter. It reminded me of a working men's club, and of the few women present they all looked as if they'd rather be elsewhere.

I told Graham about my weekend in the country.

"It always happens. They're just being friendly," Graham said.

The following week James took me to a pub in which most of the drinkers were native speakers. The atmosphere had pasted itself to the faces of the larger than life personalities sitting in the shaded booths with sticky beer drenched tables. It was an American themed pub with the Stars and Stripes hung on a wooden pole above the bar, bleached of its colors. The man behind the bar spoke with a hint of American, but clearly Polish.

"I was there when Clinton got his dick sucked," he informed a woman ordering a brightly colored cocktail.

There was a laminated ketchup smeared menu with hamburgers and French Fries and Budweiser advertised, and several glass framed portraits of American presidents hung on the walls. Pride of place was given over to a ten inch bust of Pope John Paul II standing on a shelf in a corner above the cognac bottles, his strange conical hat yellow from all the cigarette smoke. All of the windows in the pub were blacked out, giving the exterior the appearance of what they called in Warsaw, 'a gentlemen's club.'

Graham introduced a woman leaning against a pinball machine called Christine. She was unattractively thin, with one skeletal hand tapping restlessly on the glass surface of the machine... rat-a-tat, rat-a-tat.

"You drag this poor sod along for one of your legendary introductory pub crawls, Graham?"

"Leave him alone, he's not one of your head cases."

"Pity."

Graham went to the bar.

"Which school are you at? I'm with Metropolitan," she said.

She could have been anywhere between twenty-five and thirty-five. Her mousy hair looked damp in the light.

"Study English," I replied.

"Never heard of it."

"How long have you been in Warsaw?"

She rolled her eyes scornfully.

"Obviously longer than you have."

"Sorry?"

"I daresay you will be soon enough."

"Is this your shtick for the new natives speakers?"

"Jesus, you're sensitive."

She stepped towards me and I flinched, but she merely put her hand on my shoulder, smiling in a way that wasn't meant to endear her to me.

"You better leave Warsaw while you have the chance," she said.

"What?"

She cupped the back of my neck and pulled me forward so that her nose was inches from mine. Graham was looking at me from the bar and almost imperceptibly shaking his head not to argue with her.

"Go home to your family. Go back before you begin to really see."

She let go of my neck and walked away, across the pub and into the ladies. I glanced at Graham who lifted his shoulders as if to say 'whoops.'

(5)

I decided to visit the Warsaw Uprising museum. If anything could offer change, I was positive the museum could. I heard a German woman speaking on her cell phone in the queue ahead of me. She kept looking at her feet while speaking, which made me uneasy.

Inside the museum I peered into its rooms as children do when monitoring their parents covertly, not at all confident of what I might find. There was a communications depot with mannequins poised at tables laden with wireless equipment. A memorial wall, covered in hundreds of black and white photographs, was a monolith among the tourists. I bought a ticket for a short film about the destruction of Warsaw and sat in a screening room with 3D glasses as a plane flew over a desolate landscape that had somehow once been the capital. A flock of birds flapped below us, smoky forms, conspicuous above the ravaged landscape.

I sat on a bench near the memorial wall, listening to the people, understanding something of what they were saying, but my limited Polish precluded me from most of it. It was a relief not knowing, and just looking into the faces of some of those faces said a lot more than any of the captioned photographs could. I left with images of people blurred by time, no different than the people waiting in the queues as I was leaving. I squinted against the sunlight and hurried for my tram.

When I returned to my apartment I discovered a frame print above the sofa crookedly protruding from the wall because the six inch nail which supported it was too large for the hole. A trail of plaster dust covered the back of the sofa. It was an unremarkable painting showing a peasant woman standing in a bank of snow. I'd never met the landlord as he dealt directly with the school instead of me, who deducted rent and bills from my wages. I liked the arrangement, but knowing he'd been in the apartment without my permission made that comfort feel illusory.

I made some tea and lay on the sofa reading a book. I couldn't concentrate. I put the book down and looked at the picture hanging above me. I stood up and took the picture down. Behind it on the wall written in ballpoint, in Polish, were the words JESLI TU ZOSTANIESZ. I checked my Polish dictionary. The translation read: *If you stay here.*

(6)

At the end of July when the intensive language course finished I decided to leave Warsaw and it was Graham who helped set up an interview for me with a smaller school in the south west of the country.

"I worked there five years ago. Nice town, you'll like it there, the people are decent."

There was a forty minute telephone interview with a woman called Julia, swiftly followed by a verbal agreement that on provision of references and TEFL documentation scanned and emailed to them, I had the job. She emailed the same day to tell me the new semester would start at the beginning of August. The day before we were to finish classes I told Anna I was moving on.

"We might not be able to get a replacement for you so quickly," she argued.

I pointed out that nobody in the school had spoken to me about the new semester.

"Besides, the summer will give you plenty of time to find a new teacher."

"I said replacement, not substitute."

I thought it pointless trying to explain the difference to her.

I spent my last weekend in Warsaw drinking with James. I told him what Chrissy had said in the American themed pub shortly after introducing her.

"Why didn't you mention it earlier?"

"She was hovering round all evening. I thought she might be a mate of yours."

"Forget her, mate. Typical native speaker casualty that one."

He murmured ambiguous criticisms about her being like a lightning rod for 'your sort,' whatever that meant, but I didn't ask what that might translate into.

On Monday I took a direct train to Zielona Gora. It was a five hour journey in which I sat on my suitcase in the corridor outside one of the carriages, forever having to stand up every ten minutes to let people get past to the toilet. When I arrived a middle-aged woman stood waiting for me in the train station holding up a sign with my name written on it. She smiled when she saw me, which automatically disappeared once we were outside and heading to her car. She told me her name was Julia, the woman who'd interviewed me on the phone.

"I am the school secretary," she said.

I wondered if she really was the woman I'd spoken to in the phone interview because her English was of a considerably lower quality by comparison.

"Our boss calls me the coordinator," she laughed, "but she does not pay me enough money, so I am really secretary." In her car she made the expected small talk which soon petered out into a nervous silence. She made the occasional comment, angrily gesturing at the other drivers trying to overtake her. She pointed out a fountain with some statutes, couples walking through the fading light of the afternoon, as if civilization were unknown to me. The buildings were more colorful than those of Warsaw, playgrounds among avenues of trees, random stone benches set back against hedgerows. We entered a hilly district of residential blocks and min-supermarkets, and twenty-minutes later I was standing in the middle of my new apartment. Julia left me to unpack promising to return around eight so she could take me to meet the other new arrivals. She was dour enough to turn the most convivial atmosphere sour within minutes, and I was glad when she was gone.

The apartment was unnaturally spacious for one person. Somebody had had the idea of turning the apartment into an imitation of a hunting lodge, the walls overlaid with dark wooden panels, the ceiling pinned with replica logs. More alarmingly, there were a dozen or so animal skulls nailed to the walls throughout the apartment. I inspected them to help determine their species, but none of them looked familiar.

In the bedroom, above the fold out sofa, was a rectangular glass-framed painting of the Last Supper, which was the width of the entire doorway. It dominated the room. I thought about taking it down, but eventually decided to leave it where it was. I was afraid of what I might find written on the wall behind it. For years I'd floated uncaringly between agnosticism and atheism, yet strangely it didn't offend my usual intolerance for religion.

I found a note in English from Julia which led me to a bag of frozen pierogi in the fridge, some fresh bread rolls on the kitchen countertop and a dozen cans of tinned peaches in the cupboards above an old fashioned cooker. Out of the kitchen window I could see evergreens which was strangely reassuring. I'd tried making a mental note of the route Monika had taken me, but all I recalled of the journey were the closeness of the streets and that Zielona Gora appeared to be in the midst of a great forested area. I thought my new surroundings would romanticize things for me. It'd happened in Gijon, before the accident, so why not here?

I met Julia outside my block as instructed and when she appeared I climbed into the back of the car as there was a young woman sitting in the front passenger seat.

"Hey there," I said, adopting my most convincing greeting.

"Adrianna," she said, extending her hand across the back seat. She had short black hair cut at angle to her cheekbones, heavily studded earlobes that flashed in the light and no make-up except for her nails which she'd painted blue. I guessed she was in her late twenties, or at the very least, a few years younger than me.

As we drove out of the estate Adrianna reeled off the usual TEFL teacher story of the places she'd been – Lisbon, Munich – while also informing me that she was originally from Hyde in Manchester, but for the past five years had been living in Edinburgh with her boyfriend since doing her Masters Degree in applied linguistics.

"TEFL seemed like as good a way as any of putting some real distance between him and me."

We both laughed and Julia gave us a puzzled look, but remained silent.

Despite the jaunty exterior she showed, Adrianna had a quiet hesitancy about her, which was why I took the opportunity to relate half the details of my life before reaching the town centre. The sheer enormity of my descriptions as I relayed the stark minutiae of half remembered acts, helped transform them into outrageous stunts, and so mythologizing myself into somebody I would ever wish to be. The whole time I was speaking, Adrianna wore a bemused expression which might have meant anything, but to which I attached some importance. Meanwhile Julia didn't raise so much as an eyebrow, looking in the rearview mirror just the once. She had the look of a woman ultimately prepared for all kinds of bullshit.

We parked up in a badly lit street opposite one of the many delivery entrances to what Julia said was the national vodka factory, only with its razor wired fences looked more like a prison block.

"This street okay in the daytime, but at night, you be careful. Anybody asks for cigarette, ignore them."

We followed her, passing residential blocks standing in

the gloom.

"Not being funny, Monika, but if this is the bad part of town, what're we doing here?"

"You are okay. Come, this way."

She ducked through a low brick doorway, down a steep flight of steps, passed through a second brick doorway and into a large circular room with a bar. I could just about distinguish tables and chairs set out against the walls in the dim light.

"Here they are."

Three people came out of an alcove near the bar, greeting us with such loud cheery camaraderie it took not only me completely by surprise, but by judging from the look on her face, Adrianna appeared equally startled.

Clive and Helen, an engaged couple in their mid-twenties, introduced themselves.

"We only completed a CELTA certificate in Poznan a couple of days ago," Clive said. He must have been six feet four, yet stood next to his fiancée, who must have been at least ten inches shorter, they somehow formed a visually satisfying and symmetrical ideal.

"This is out first teaching position," Helen said.

"Crapping ourselves," Clive said, grinning good naturedly. "Have you been at it long?"

"Less than six months," I replied, "feels longer though."

"You'll be fine once you get your first lesson out of the way."

"Hello, I'm Toby."

An American man with a cheerful round face, a swathe of dark hair and wearing a Deep Purple t-shirt came at me so suddenly, I stepped back and collided with the bar.

"For a moment I thought you were somebody I owed

money," I joked.

He realized I was joking, and looked away embarrassedly.

"British humor, right. I get it."

He motioned to the barmaid to order himself another drink.

"I sincerely doubt it," Clive muttered.

Helen feigned a punch to her boyfriend's chin, and Clive jerked backwards, mocking her, or Toby, it was hard to say. I saw Adrianna give me a quick glance.

"Are they with the school?" I asked. There were a group of women on the other side of the room and I wondered if they were teachers, but since they remained seated I thought they must simply be other patrons, for our presence barely altered them, only some mild, disaffected curiosity making them turn blankly towards us every so often.

Helen, with her spiky blonde hair and distinct low voice, shrugged and turned back to the bar.

"They came with Julia before she went to pick you and Adrianna up. So I guess so."

I glanced over at the secretary, her arms folded on the bar as she waited for another drink.

"They're not Polish, are they?"

"What makes you say that?" Adrianna asked.

"Exempting bosses and hierarchy, the Polish people I've met are a sight more hospitable than most," I said. "I don't know, that lot don't strike me as being Polish. They have more in common with the people from the village where I grew up..."

For the next hour or so we stood together at the bar drinking, swapping stories, exchanging potentially useful information for any arguments that might lie ahead of us.

drank too much, especially having only eaten the packed sandwiches I'd had on the train from Warsaw. I swayed uneasily against the bar, half listening to what the others were saying. I looked across the room and saw that Julia was talking to the group of young women.

"What's wrong with them? Why don't they come and say hello?"

"Apparently, according to Julia, us native speakers have a reputation for being party animals. Some of them tend not to associate with us. Maybe that's why?"

"I'm going over," I said.

"Don't." Adrianna tried to stop me, but I was already halfway across the room.

"Hi, I'm George," I almost shouted as I reached the group. A young woman with a long pleated skirt, and a brown woolen shawl expertly worn round her shoulders, whose face said she was younger than any of us native speakers, but whose fashion sense said otherwise.

"Hello."

She rose from her seat in an unequivocal physical line, her hand thrust out at me with jerky suddenness, which I hurriedly shook and which she loosened from my grip only when I stepped back. Like her skirt and shawl, her hair was a faded corn brown, as were her eyes. I felt a cloying sense of dullness rise up between us.

"I'm one of the new native speakers."

I'd had a sarcastic monologue worked, but looking at her unsympathetic face I realized it was a lost cause before I could even begin. Over her shoulder her friends had the same expression.

"I'm Magda, I am also a teacher." She sat back down, her knees closing firmly together. Her small neat hands returned to the smooth lap of her skirt. She turned her head to indicate the others. "These are my colleagues."

I raised my hand to acknowledge them.

"Hi there," I said, feeling thoroughly foolish for persisting. The other teachers shared a similarity to that of the woman in front of me. Indifference, circumspect dislike?

"Nice meeting you," I said, "better get back to my friends."

"Yes." She looked up at me, not even blinking, just staring.

Not until I was standing at the bar with the others did I dare look over to that side of the room again. At the very least I expected my brief introduction to have stirred them into action, that they'd be talking amongst themselves. But they retained their positions, motionlessly synchronized to one another. I even had trouble working out which was the woman I'd spoken to.

"That was a success," Helen said.

"Raging," I muttered.

(7)

I recall somebody saying somewhere in the ancient past of last night: "Help me with him," maneuvering me into the back of a taxi that was waiting outside under the hazy glow of an old fashioned streetlamp. I woke up to find myself fully clothed on the sofa, change scattered all over the floor.

The rest of the previous night we'd embraced a dozen disparate topics, geography, nationality and class background among them. A good natured debate at the beginning though as we consumed more alcohol it degenerated into the common verbal skirmishes which arise out of too many personalities clamoring for attention. At one point Adrianna had put her arm round my shoulders.

"Quit, while you're ahead."

I had some breakfast, boiled perogi and a tin of peaches, not an ideal culinary start to the day. Afterwards I sat on the balcony of my apartment to read a Polish phrase book. Below my apartment a group of boys were playing army among the evergreens, their severed branches – the approximation of machine guns – sometimes indistinguishable from the branches they were hiding behind. I could see two teenage girls smoking cigarettes near a children's playground, saying very little to each other as they traced the smoke through the air. It could have been anywhere in the world, but it was England I was thinking of.

A man with a black greyhound allowed it to walk him through the woods, the dog startled by the running shapes of children in mock military stand-offs. On the balcony above mine I could smell food frying, the scrape of a pan against the hob, the clatter of utensils in a sink, a tap gushing, water turning into steam. It was a good day to rid myself of a hangover, the people in the neighborhood, the normality of their actions making me acutely aware that although I was thousands of miles from home, for once the similarity of what I was seeing didn't feel like a betrayal.

A couple of hours later Clive rang to ask if I wanted to meet everybody for a walk round the town center.

"Sure, as long as you can assure me I didn't insult anybody last night."

"Was about to ask you the same thing. Helen says not, but you know, we only met yesterday, and it's difficult knowing if you have or haven't in those kinds of situations."

"That's good enough for me," I said.

The day was overcast as long flute shaped clouds drifted

over the five of us, but it didn't seem to deter the people in the streets. There were lots of shoppers out on the crowded pavements, many of whom kept openly staring at us.

"I didn't think we native speakers stood out so much," Toby said. "You know if it were a country like Greece, or maybe Spain, people on the beach all time of the day, tanned toned and muscular, of course we lot stand out. But here's different. Yet I get the feeling they're scrutinizing us."

"Is this to do with those other teachers last night?" Helen asked.

"The people, the ones we've met so far, they seem nice, granted, a bit formal, but easy enough to get on with. But I think I'm going to tone things down a bit. Not take the piss so much, if you know what I mean," I said.

"That's what I was thinking," Toby added.

Bars filled the town square, nestled on the ground floors of what must have once been private houses, concrete yards with canopies, murals on walls and identical painted railings. Through the windows I could see people talking so animatedly I was at a complete loss to explain the teachers from the night before.

"Wish I'd brought my camera," Helen said, pointing at a pair of statues on a marble plinth, a soldier jabbing a bayoneted rifle at imaginary foes, the other a peasant woman grasping his legs.

We walked along a series of interconnecting avenues in which we discovered small museums, bistros and bakeries. An Egyptian restaurant with steamed up windows sat on a concrete island with surrounding flowerbeds, while across the street stood a theatre with a wooden exterior. A building with a grey façade, the brick underneath exposed like a subcutaneous layer, turned out to be the local cinema.

"No, multiplexes," said Clive, "is that a good or bad thing?"

It didn't take us long to walk through the town center, gothic clock towers more common than I'd have supposed, the sky slanting over the rooftops as if somebody had failed to successfully slide a box lid back in place, one end of the city overcast, the other end glaring whitely.

We came into another market square crowded with people, where there must have been at least four hundred demonstrators for what looked like a protest of some description. Nearly all of the people were elderly, most of whom were carrying banners whose painted slogans I couldn't interpret. A tall woman with bright orange hair stood on a platform behind a podium wrestling with a microphone. Rows of faces looked up at her expressionlessly, making her all the more agitated. The woman spoke into the microphone, unintelligible words to my ears. For all I knew the elderly demonstrators understood her no better with their stony faced expressions.

"They speak no sense," said a woman with a baby in a pushchair behind us. "Are you Australians?"

"English and American," Adrianna replied.

"Actually, I'm Welsh by birth," Clive said.

"You've lived in Bristol since you were five weeks old," Helen cut in.

The woman gave us a look which said she'd more important matters than to stand about talking to foreigners disputing their nationalities, before turning away with the pushchair. The baby looked up at us with an expression that said he was no more certain of what the woman with orange hair was saying than any of us were.

I looked at the faces in the crowd. Such solemnity made

them alike that they reminded me of the teachers from the night before.

"I think they've gone to sleep," Helen noted.

The woman brought the microphone nearer to her face, the words she kept uttering unobtrusively dull by the lack of a reaction from the crowd, but still, I remained convinced they were the same words.

Toby stood in front of me peering at a phrase book, with Adrianna leaning over his shoulder.

"I think that's it," Toby said, "it sounds like that's what she's saying."

"Saying what?" I asked.

"It sounds like 'instead of us.'"

I thought of the words on the wall of my old apartment in Warsaw.

We soon grew bored of waiting for something to happen and decided to continue our walk. We followed an alleyway that shrank so narrowly we had to turn sideway as a priest in a cloak pushed past, his eyes squeezing together, blanking us out. The sky overhead dwindled to a monochromatic thread. We came across a clock-repair shop, its windows full of old brass carriage clocks, swinging ornamented hands against the cloth draped display, and for no reason I could explain I wished I'd had a reason to go inside to listen to them tick.

(8)

On Monday we arrived at the school in the early afternoon to find the place completely empty except for Julia. The secretary explained a slow start to the academic year meant classes wouldn't be starting until the next week. She decided we should all take the opportunity to familiarize ourselve with the school and its policies.

84

MOUNTAINS OF SMOKE

She took us through our contracts paragraph by paragraph, all of which was in Polish, so we had to take her word for it. She gave each of us a red binder with the words SCHOOL PHILOSOPHY stenciled on the front. There was a five page pamphlet inside detailing what was expected of us as teachers. The word 'cooperation' came up more than once. After we'd ploughed through all of the paperwork she showed us round the premises. As we were looking at the classrooms, Julia opened a door.

"Staff room."

There were no windows, but yellow breeze block walls with work cubicles.

"It's a bit like a call center," Clive pointed out. He had a guitar with him in its cover, and hoisted it to the other shoulder as he peered round the room.

Julia nodded cheerfully, not understanding what he meant.

"What about the other teachers?" I asked.

"They go downstairs," she said, changing the subject so swiftly it showed on each of our faces, "I will have your timetables ready in twenty minutes. I will speak to each of you independently. Toby you are first."

"I'm going for a cigarette," I said, thinking to myself that the only thing missing from the teachers' room were plastic slop out buckets.

(9)

A man in a navy blue dinner jacket walked up to me outside the school entrance as I was having my cigarette.

"You one of the new native speakers?" he asked.

He stank of alcohol, his eyes ringed by dark circles. He rubbed a hand over his skull as if searching for evidence of his thoughts, or the point of their exit.

"Yes. You okay?" I shouldn't have asked the question because some of the alertness that no doubt characterized this face slipped into his eyes, giving them purpose.

"I left at Christmas," he said, ignoring my question. He looked up at the school, which occupied the fourth floor of a former post office building which was at the center of the main business district. The heat was stifling, and yet standing next to this man I felt conspicuous in my combats, short-sleeved white cotton shirt and sandals.

He was what the younger TEFL teachers often referred to as the Old Brigade, middle-aged, borderline alcoholics with incalculable neuroses who'd come to Poland as Communism had departed. Once he'd have been a rock star of social interest at a time when there were hardly any Westerners living in their country. Twenty years later these dinosaurs of the private school industry endlessly complained of the shoddy, ill-dressed kids who'd flooded the country and given Englishmen a bad name.

"They not pay you?" It was the right kind of question to ask. The private school industry in Europe, especially central Europe and further eastwards, could be dubious in its dealings with people they sometimes assumed would be only passing through, and therefore easy enough to short change.

"If only," he laughed. "Can I have one of those?" He pointed at my cigarette.

"Sure." I gave him one, and he lit it with shaky hands a he grasped my disposable lighter.

"I'm Kevin Buchan."

Sweat covered his fingertips, and I had to suppress th urge to wipe my hand on my combats.

"Has she told you about the replacements?"

"The replacements? Substitute teachers?"

He looked at the cigarette in his hand.

"I'm scared of going home, you know. Back to Britain. Scared it'll be different."

His face changed suddenly as if remembering he was speaking to a complete stranger.

"Listen, I've got to go. But thanks for the cigarette."

He walked to the corner of the street and looked back. I waved to him, but somebody in an estate agents, a tall woman in a white blouse knocked on the window to beckon him inside. He shook his head, but she opened the door and leaned out to say something to him as a removal van momentarily obscured the pair of them. When the van had motored to the end of the street, both the woman and Kevin Buchan were gone.

(10)

"Another week without work, I think I can get used to this life," said Clive.

Helen slapped him on the arm.

"Typical fella," she laughed.

We were walking to Toby's apartment, who led the way through a series of winding cobbled streets carrying a bag of lager.

"You up for this jam?" Toby asked Clive, and looking at me, "do you play an instrument George?"

"Afraid not. Why, are you both musicians?"

"I play bass," Toby said, blushing.

Clive lifted one shoulder to cast a surprised look at the guitar hanging there. Toby didn't seem to know what was so funny, his expression once again that of the perpetually doomed.

"I'm a postgraduate musician believe it or not, but work is scarce on the ground these days for session musicians, hence the old TEFL get out of jail card."

Clive told me about his guitars, his collection of records, his obsession with Mark E Smith, which Helen said was a form of obsessive compulsive disorder.

"She's jealous she'd only got her knitting," he said.

"You knit?" Adrianna asked, genuinely impressed.

"Put it this way, if you need some daft bobble hat for the winter, give me a call. If you want a respectable cardigan, forget it"

"I think it's admirable," Toby said with total seriousness, "my grandmother used to knit, but my mum or my sisters don't know how."

"Do you knit?" I asked, instantly regretting exposing him in such a way.

"I didn't mean it to sound like," he mumbled.

"I know what you were getting at." Helen poked him in the ribs because he was wearing an expression which said he felt people were picking on him.

The apartment was smaller than my place, on the second floor of a block overlooking an outdoor flea market. There was the usual wall encompassing wardrobe, the staple of furniture in apartments rented out by elderly Polish landlords. The décor was only slightly better than my place but there were no animal skulls on the walls and a flat screen television.

"I've got a little something," Clive said, taking a puff on an imaginary joint. "I forgot I even had it until I was unpacking my things. It was in the bottom of my rucksack."

"You were lucky they didn't go through your bags at the airport."

"That's what Helen said."

I opened the balcony door and stepped outside, Clive following me.

"I don't really smoke," I said.

"Which means sometimes."

"Do you smoke?"

Toby was hovering behind us as if he wasn't quite sure where to stand.

"Time to time." He gave me a look I couldn't work out. "You guys want some beers? he asked.

"Yep, sure," said Clive, peering over the edge of the balcony railings, "we've got an audience."

A gang of boys stood on the edge of the curb watching us. Clive waved, but they refused to return the greeting..

"Dzien dobra," Clive yelled, but his Polish failed to rouse them either. He repeated the words and I wanted to tell him to stop, but after a minute he gave up, seeing it was having no effect. "They must have heard us talking English," he said by way of explanation.

We went back inside and Clive picked up Toby's bass laid across the end of the sofa, running his fingers up the frets.

"Don't leave it like this," he shouted through to the kitchen, "you'll end up knackering it, Toby."

"He's not as anal as you," Helen shouted back.

In the kitchen Helen and Adrianna were smoking cigarettes and drinking wine.

"Oooh, posh," I teased, trying to hide my surprise that Adrianna smoked.

"Just like being back in uni," Helen said.

Toby passed me a beer.

"Party's in the kitchen as always." Clive appeared in the

doorway, taking one of the beers Toby was offering.

"This was restricted to girls' only," Helen said.

"You said I was an honoree woman."

"Only when it suits me sweetheart." She winked at him and raised her glass. "To us having a good laugh."

"To changing," Adrianna said.

I couldn't tell if it were the words or the thought that I was on the verge of asking her out somewhere, but I felt suddenly very nervous.

"Give me the weed," Helen said, her glass of wine spilling as she put one arm round Clive's shoulders, her free hand snaking down his chest and into his jeans pockets. "Bingo," she grinned. "Go and play your music while we do something far more productive." She removed her hand and showed Adrianna a square packet with a lump of resin. "Adrianna, you any good at skinning up?"

"Useless," she replied.

Was that a quick glance to see if I approved or not?

"Want me to do it?" Clive asked.

"You must be joking, you're worse than me."

They reminded me of a couple scripted in sitcom language, beneath the surface of which their relationship was that of two strangers accidentally thrown together because of the roles they played.

Toby disappeared into his bedroom and returned with a small amp. Clive unzipped the cover to his guitar as he followed Toby, revealing a semi-acoustic. After a moment I could smell the aroma of the resin drifting in from the kitchen. Clive began tuning up his guitar as Adrianna came in with a joint. She lit it and passed it to Toby who held it between his lips, the bass guitar poking out one hand.

"We should try buckets later," Clive said.

Toby expelled a lungful of air and said: "I'm game."

"I'll shut the balcony door," I said.

"Shit, yeah, what if the neighbors smell it?" Clive asked. "Do you think they'd call the police? Can you imagine that? Foreign teachers arrested for possession of resin. They have a zero tolerance policy in this country. It's not like back home."

I stopped in the middle of the room, the balcony door forgotten about. Toby passed the joint to Clive who stuck it in the corner of his mouth as if impersonating a youthful Keith Richards. He started to laugh, struggling to keep hold of the acoustic, the joint dribbling ash onto floor.

"Fuck off, I haven't even had a drag on it and you're already making me paranoid," I said.

"Maybe you're stoned just on the smoke," Toby said, "Really susceptible or something."

There was a glimmer in his eyes, a self-congulatory nod at his quick wit.

"I just haven't bothered with it," I replied.

"Here then, its yours."

I took a drag and felt a tickle irritatingly worm its way through my chest, and coughed for several seconds. When I looked up I expected to see Toby grinning at me but he was in the kitchen talking to Adrianna and Helen.

(II)

"Have half, that way you won't do a whitey on us," Clive said, seeing the expression on my face.

"I'm okay, I can handle it. "But when Adrianna giggled I felt the urge to escape the bathroom. Everybody else had had a *bucket bong* as Clive kept referring to it, and the homemade contraption seemed like a minor work of engineering brilliance to everyone except me, the empty two-liter plastic bottle of Coke with its bottom half sawn off, a flap of tinfoil expertly molded round the mouth of the bottle, sitting in a mop-bucket of water.

"Pass me the resin," Helen said.

Clive gave her the brown cube which had been significantly larger not more than twenty minutes ago. Helen held it to the flame of my disposable lighter, a tiny curl of smoke giving off a fragrant aroma. Helen crumbled some of the resin onto the tinfoil, covering the pinpricks in the silver material.

"Ready?" Clive patted me on the shoulder. Toby hovered in the corridor, unconcealed delight on his face.

"Go on," I said.

As Helen lit the resin she forced the bottle down into the water, and thick dirty smoke swirled against the rippling plastic. I leaned over and took hold of it in one hand.

"Careful, don't squeeze it too hard, or you'll force the air back up."

I relaxed my grip, feeling the heat coming through the plastic and bent over mouth of the bottle. Helen quickly removed the tinfoil, and placed her hand over the opening to trap the smoke inside.

"Inhale as much as you can, but remember to hold it for a few seconds."

I sucked in as hard as I could, my lungs swelling like balloons. I pictured Toby's grinning face and before I could think of anything else, I exhaled the smoke, spluttering as saliva ran down my chin.

"Jesus," I moaned.

"Did you see that? He took the whole lot. From now on this man here shall be known as Iron Lungs."

MOUNTAINS OF SMOKE

My vision had become a screen of grey filmic shapes, accompanied by a series of disembodied voices.

"Let's get her racked up again," Toby challenged.

I walked out of the bathroom and into the living room to the sound of tiny applause. Everything looked the same, but the air was stale and smoky. Was I going to be sick? I didn't think so. The noise from the bathroom was a distant conference of words. I sat on the back of the sofa, not trusting myself to get too comfortable.

"You okay, George?" Adrianna flopped onto the sofa.

"You?" I asked.

She reached up and grabbed the leg of my jeans.

"You're too far away George," she laughed.

I slid down beside her, her hip touching mine.

"That's better," she said.

I looked at her.

"Are you sure you're alright?"

"Of course."

Helen came into the room, coughing.

"I'm not. I'm fried."

Adrianna jerked backwards at the sound of Helen's voice.

Clive and Toby entered the room laughing.

"Anybody want a beer?" Toby seemed to yell.

"I'll have one," Clive said, strumming a tune on his acoustic.

"Fancy a cig?" Helen asked.

"Are you talking to me?" I asked.

"No, Adrianna," she smiled.

Helen raised her eyebrows questioningly.

Toby reentered the room with the beer.

"Almost out," he said.

"There's a shop downstairs. George will come with me,

won't you?" Clive asked.

"Sure."

Toby muttered as he pulled the ring tab to his beer. Helen laughed and Adrianna stood up and walked into the kitchen. The speed of the conversation was becoming too fast for me. I got up off the sofa and before I had much memory of doing so, Clive and I were outside blinking against the sun.

"I ask you a question, George?"

There were a string of small shops on the ground floor of the block, as was the custom with residential areas. If we'd had to walk any further I might have turned back. My head was swimming with sounds and noises. Clive's voice was an anchor in the muddiness of my thoughts.

"Sounds like you're going to get personal."

"You mind?"

"I'll tell you after you've asked."

"Do you fancy Adrianna?"

"Are you asking, or is that Toby checking out the lay of the land."

"Toby? No, he hasn't said a thing."

I'd given myself away.

"Yes, I like her. I mean I've only just met her though."

"Take it from me, you'd be a fool not to ask her out."

"Is it the effects of your drugs, or have we just traveled back in time to when I was fourteen?"

"Never too young for a holiday romance."

"Holiday?"

"I don't plan on doing this for more than a year. It's a good laugh and everything, but I'm not going to end up doing this in my late forties slumming it with gap year students, pretending I'm a proper teacher and all that shit."

I thought of Kevin Buchan.

"Though saying that, there are worse ways to see the world."

There was an affability to Clive which hadn't been there before. My head was reeling in so many different directions I had to point at the door of the off-license to stop myself blurting out the running commentary in my head.

"Let's brave the paranoia," I said.

My heartbeat became a prominent thudding in my chest, intensifying from the sound of Clive's words to the face of the two women behind the counter. One was stacking shelves from atop a metal ladder, the other was sitting on a stool behind an old fashioned till. Crates of bottled beer and several large wall coolers displaying cans took up most of the space in the shop. The thought that our nationality might serve as some form of entertainment for the locals had sounded unlikely when Clive had mentioned it earlier, but the woman on the ladder inclined her head over one shoulder and grimaced at the sound of our voices. The other woman stood up and visibly stiffened. I could see Clive thought the same thing as me, that we should just turn around and abandon our plans. In our state the entire experience would feel excruciatingly longer than it would.

Before I could say anything Clive spoke to the woman behind the till. His Polish wasn't perfect, but it was better than mine. The woman on the ladder looked down at him and smiled. The assistant behind the till nodded appreciatively and opened one of the coolers and put two six packs on the counter.

"That should do us." He paid for the beer and gave one six pack to me to carry.

When we left the shop the kids were back again, about

eight of them this time, standing on the edge of the curb again, directly below the balcony of Toby's apartment. They watched us, their heads moving inquisitively as if we were a mythological many headed creature. The paranoia kicked in again, and I wondered if they'd been waiting round the corner, hiding from us?

"They're hardly covert," Clive said, pressing the intercom buzzer. Helen's voice emerged, but it sounded as if it were echoing out of a tunnel, and he was about to answer when a stone hit the top of the door and rebounded onto the pavement. We turned to see the kids run off down the street.

"Here, take these." Clive shoved the other six pack into my arms. "Little bastards."

"Don't mate, just leave them."

"Hello? Hello?" Helen's voice pricked the bubble I felt I was in as I watched Clive turn a corner and disappear after the kids.

"Your boyfriend's just run off after a gang of kids."

"Is this a wind-up, George?"

I could hear the change in her, rushed by the uncertainty of what I was telling her.

"No."

"For fuck's sake."

"What's wrong?"

"He's got a rotten temper on him, that's what. A kid clocked him with a stone couple years back. It's been bugging him ever since. Can you go see where he is? I'm coming down."

Now I remembered why I hadn't smoked anything in years. It simply wasn't worth the hassle of second guessing not only yourself, but everybody else's actions, too.

I walked to the corner of the street. Two large sweaty men were hauling bags of coal from the back of a truck, but there was no sign of Clive or the boys.

Helen came running round the corner.

"I hope he doesn't do anything daft."

"Those lads have been outside the apartment all day."

"All day?"

"I mean since we got here."

"Were they just sitting there on the curb and looking up at the window, not saying anything?"

"You saw them?"

"Not these ones."

"Obviously. Where was this?"

"After we got home from the welcoming party. I was having a quick cigarette on the balcony, and there were these boys sitting outside our block. I thought it was strange because it was past three in the morning."

"Clive never mentioned it."

"He was passed out on the sofa like always."

"They're probably intrigued by us lot."

"Why would you say that?"

"I didn't, it was Clive, but he's probably right."

"This is Central Europe, George, not sub-Sahara Africa. There are plenty of English speaking foreigners in this country. Clive has the idea people are going to love us or something simply because we're Westerners."

The anxiety had left her eyes, replaced by disappointment or something that went deeper.

"If you ask me, it's just lads being lads. Just because we're abroad, don't expect people to be any different."

"Do you want me to go and look for him?"

"Leave him to it. He'll be back in a minute after they've

run him ragged."

Back in the flat Helen stood on the balcony smoking a cigarette, acting like she wasn't really appearing for her fiancé to reappear, which he shortly did.

"Where the hell have you been?" she yelled over the balcony.

I heard Clive's voice coming from below, but couldn't make out what he was saying. Helen came in off the balcony, her face a pale reflection of what it was only moments ago. She looked at me as the buzzer sounded.

"I'll let him in," Toby said.

Helen detached one of the cans from the six-pack as casually as possible, but I could see something was wrong with her. She followed Toby into the corridor as he opened the front door. I could hear Clive's approaching footsteps on the stairwell. For the second time that day my heartbeat became conspicuous. Clive's face bobbed into view as he mounted the last flight of stairs. When he saw Helen he smiled in such a way as if he hadn't seen her in hours. He stepped through the doorway and I looked at Helen, but she too was smiling, and it was this most of all which frightened me. Behind the smile, behind those eyes, she was screaming.

(12)

The next morning Clive rang just before midday asking if I wanted to come round his place to play cards with everybody. I told him I was still suffering the effects from the night before.

"Are you okay, mate?" He sounded like Clive, though had to remind myself I barely knew anything about him. I'd spent all morning trying to convince myself I hadn't seen anything peculiar in Helen's behavior yesterday, nor with

Clive for that matter. The combination of alcohol and resin had thrown me what Toby referred to as a *curve ball*, or as Adrianna had presumed, *a whitey*. But speaking to Clive on the phone did nothing to alleviate the strangeness I kept glimpsing, as if somebody were tentatively allowing me to see more than permitted.

"We were all wasted," he laughed, "though cooked is probably a better description."

"Next time I'm sticking to a couple of cans, that's it," I said.

"If you change your mind, call us. I'm sure Adrianna would be chuffed."

When the film finished I decided to go for a walk, but once outside I couldn't rid myself of the feeling I'd crossed some invisible boundary, that I was trespassing, only I couldn't see any signs or notices telling me so.

I walked through the neighborhood, the other blocks exactly the same as my own. Two old women on a bench asked me something in a language I could have sworn wasn't Polish. I smiled, shook my head and hurried past. After a hundred yards I realized they were following me. *They're only heading in the same direction.* I turned onto a concrete path, children's bicycles thrown on the ground in front of me, more old people watching me walk by. Across an open grassy space between four smaller blocks, the ground was littered with fragmented bricks. The neighborhood came to an abrupt end. I stood at the top of a grassless slope looking east, a basketball court at the bottom, the wire of its fence curled away from the rusting poles holding it all together, looking like collapsed butterfly nets. A girl of about fifteen stood in the court all by herself practicing with a football. The ball kept missing the hoop, thwacking loudly against the board. Beyond the court a nondescript building stood in a yellowing field, a few knurled trees, some of which were no higher than the teenage girl, poked their branches above the grass. I cupped my eyes and squinted. The area sailed into greyness against the contrariness of the blue summer sky, no blocks or signs of roads, only the edge of the forest which encircled the town. I strained to pick up anything other than the thwack of the ball hitting the board above the basketball hoop. I hadn't walked that far, yet I felt as if I'd entered an incomplete place, one in which normality was a thin skein ripping at the seams.

I swung round on my heels, bright sunshine playing off windows, making the shadows dance. I spotted a man stood in the entrance to one of the blocks, the glint of his glasses. He mightn't have been watching me, but when I considered the drab scenery I thought that unlikely. I felt compelled to raise my hand to see how he'd react. Would it be like looking at a reflection? I could no longer hear the sound of the basketball hitting the board above the hoop. The girl in the court stood watching me as the figure in the doorway stepped outside. I moved along the top of the slope, and jogged into the courtyard of a modern block. A pallet of bricks sat on the ground. The windows of the apartments were bare, dusty from recent completion. New blocks waiting for their occupants. My footsteps echoed after me as I ran out of the courtyard and into a street whose road was unfinished. Its pavement inclined to the gutter. A half circle of trees stood to my right where the other side of the street should have been, a meridian of broken concrete piled with rubble. The feeling that I'd strayed where I shouldn't was overwhelming. Memories of Gijon, senseless one night stands, people in the street looking or acting differently came back to me as if released from captivity. I remembered the woman in the pub in Warsaw warning me to go home before it was too late, the words written on the wall of my flat, the teachers at the welcoming party, that Clive had acted in a way that had scared the absolute hell out of Helen.

As if to compound my growing paranoia a group of boys appeared on the other side of the trees. I could easily have walked on without anybody knowing I was there, only I couldn't, immobilized with fascination. There in that unfinished section of street I watched as they drew parallel, moving forward like a troop of lost scouts searching for the familiarity of a trail, restless, chattering amongst themselves the way young boys do. They threw stones into the air, wielded sticks and wrestled with one another, noisily demonstrative of their gender. They reminded me of rope swings in woods, homemade Halloween costumes, the interminable wait for Christmas and old school photographs gathering dust in attics.

In particular they reminded me of a summer I went camping with friends who had long ago disappeared into adulthood. There'd been a wooded lot a quarter of a mile from my house and it was there we'd pitched our tent. There were a hundred other places throughout Chapel Hill similar to it, and for all we knew that day there might have been a hundred other boys our age doing exactly the same thing. We stayed up the entire night talking of girls we'd seen from distances but had never had the courage to speak to, cracking jokes at one another's expense and jumping exaggeratedly at every noise we heard. When daylight appeared, our faces blackened like charcoal from the smoke of the camp fire, we crawled inside our shabby little tent. We slept contentedly until ten in the morning, when a light fizzing rain caused the remains of our fire to smolder pathetically. To this day I still remember the frayed strap on my rucksack, the tinfoil from the sandwiches my mother had made me and which I molded into pellets and flicked into the fire, and most of all I remember the sweet, wet smell of the greenery.

I was suddenly angry for having allowed a few curious locals to get the better of me. Once I had my bearings I found my block within a relatively short time, marching back with a defiant expression. In my flat I thought about ringing the others, but the word, *replacement,* hung before me like a pulsing warning sign in garish neon. I decided against going out, even with the temptation of having the chance to speak to Adrianna.

Had Buchan meant substitutes? He couldn't have meant anything else.

I stayed home and watched Polish TV – the same as British TV, only verbally incomprehensible – and all the while I couldn't help wondering whether or not there really were subtle changes taking place, not only in the people, but also with myself.

(13)

The phone-call came at three in the morning and I woke with a panicky jolt knowing what it meant.

"George?"

"Mum? What is it? What's wrong?"

She started to sob, a horrible sound of barely controlled gulps and exhalations. I could see her standing in an anonymous hospital corridor beneath florescent lights which cruelly exposed her face, a small and vulnerable woman without anybody to distract her from the unavoidable truth of that moment.

"They've replaced him," she said.

The sound of her voice hacked away through my drowsiness and set my heart pounding. I put my hand against the wall above my bed to steady myself.

"Did you hear me, George, I said they couldn't save him. Your father, he's dead, George."

(14)

We buried my father on a Friday afternoon, a day of contrasting weather, blazing sun and heavy rain, wet pavements and drying grass among the headstones in the graveyard. I recognized very few of the people in the church, not that I paid them much attention. Organizing everything since getting back from Poland earlier in the week had exhausted me, and I remember feeling irritated when my mother started wailing uncontrollably as my father's friends lifted his coffin onto their shoulders. Lowering it into the hole she became even more hysterical, a detonation of howling, an aftershock of sudden realization. She flung her arms outwards as if caught in a blast, and I had to restrain her from doing something I could only imagine happening in the melodrama of a daytime TV show. The people round the graveside only nodded their sympathy.

At the wake I couldn't quite figure out if they were waiting for me to do something drastic, or if they themselves were uncertain. I'd no doubt they were replacements, a feeling which intensified so strongly I left my mother in the company of great aunt Jean, a seventy-year old woman from my father's side of the family who'd all the sensitivity of a police interrogator employing merciless techniques. I didn't dare look any of them in the eye as I walked into the hallway to get my coat. They were probably wondering if I'd finally tired of the pretense. I calmly opened the front door, stepped outside onto the driveway and lit a cigarette. Earlier on I'd observed my great aunt Jean talking to my father's oldest brother, Andrew, uncaring that she was in the middle of a funeral while she loudly berating him for his lack of phonecalls to his now deceased younger sibling.

"Don't make that face with me. I know for a fact you didn't bother much these past years."

I'd have intervened for the sake of my mother, except my one remaining parent had transformed into somebody else. Leaving her with aunt Jean suited my purposes. Aunt Jean be my decoy, but remembering the way she'd stalked Peter across the room as he made a pointless retreat, I realized I wasn't entirely on my own.

The worst thing about the afternoon was having to consider the possibility a heart attack hadn't killed my father. Had he woken up one morning to discover the woman lying in bed beside him wasn't the same one he'd been married to all these years, despite her looking exactly the same? I imagined my father reaching out a hand to stroke back a lock of graying hair from her forehead, when her eyes had flickered open and showed him something he was never meant to have witnessed. He might have recoiled, making it fatally obvious, or maybe he'd played along with the impostor until, exhausted by the deception, he dropped the artifice for confrontation.

Thinking about him in this way made me cry and when I walked back inside the house I sensed their curiosity because up until now I hadn't shown them anything, had refused to give them a clue as to my real feelings. They'd robbed me of the chance to mourn openly, and because of them, especially the replacement who was pretending to b my mother, they'd forced me to act in a way that was clearly less human than they were.

I found my replacement mother in the dining room arranging sandwiches on a plate. My cousin Anne was with her, and when she saw me coming she muttered inaudibly to the woman who looked exactly like my mother.

"Mother, stop fussing over everything and everyone," I said, struggling to sound reasonable.

My cousin put a hand on my mother's elbow.

"George is right, Liz. I can do them."

This other Liz gave me a teary glance. She was expecting me to comfort her, to say something conclusive to show I was no nearer to guessing she was a replacement. She continued moving objects across the surface of the buffet table, shifting plates of cold cuts from one end to the other, changing the position of the salt seller for the butter dish, an increasingly frenzied pace of sleight of hand. It'd never occurred to me how my real mother might have acted in the event of my father's death, but the replacement intimated her with unnerving authenticity.

"Mother," I said, looking down at her hands on the tablecloth, the gold band of her wedding ring glinting.

I didn't expect that she would overact again so soon after the other attempts she'd made, but before I could step out of the way or say anything to stop her, she whirled round and buried her head against my chest. I hesitated before putting my arms round her, just so everybody would know. I could hear aunt Jean still going on at Andrew, and Anne made an expression that meant it was no surprise until she realized where she was and politely, even for one of them, turned away and averted her stare. Despite the falsity of this thing spilling tears against my shirt I felt warmed by its persistence to emote what my mother would also have done. I couldn't deny they shared emotions similar to ours, which made the thought of them replacing us all the more bewildering.

A few days before I'd walked into the village to pick out a wreath from Wendy's Florists. Of the people I passed in the street I'd wondered how many of them had felt as if they were moving through a field of sensitive tripwires? How many had played their parts with a fear so consummate that within this slow street ballet of discreet movement in which one tiny gesture, one seemingly innocuous comment, could explode the artificiality. Both groups reflected one another's strategies, holding our masks in place in a game of show and tell.

I looked at the replacement's face which in some ways was more recognizable than my own. She smiled, a stringent expression, one I'd never have associated with my real mother. She squirmed out of my arms, reminding me of a toddler fleeing the sticky embrace of an overzealous grandmother.

Ever since the yachting accident in Gijon I'd learned to accept that self-sacrifice on my part would only ever be accidental, never instinctive. When my student Laura had failed to turn up for her lessons I told myself it was a tactical maneuver on her part, that being in the same room as each other would have been an emotional collusion neither of us would have wanted. We'd seen death close-up, and despite it being as drearily nondescript as everything else, it'd made us complicit. But the truth was I'd made no effort to help Laura, her father or any of their friends get the rescued sailors onboard the yacht. Had it been fear? I thought it was more like willful persistence that I should stay seated, not get in the way. But I had felt outright terror at the thought I could ever so easily slip on the slicked surface of the yacht and fall overboard, unnoticed, one more bloated corpse for the coastguard to retrieve later on that day?

So when I grabbed the replacement and held her at arm's length, tightening my grip on the flabby muscles of her arms, I told myself this was a courageous act to make up for my cowardice in Gijon.

"I know what you did," I screamed at her, and I began to shake her violently.

(15)

Somebody had left a message on the wall of the Co-op in the village in green spray paint. *NOW DO YOU SEE?* I ignored it, or at least acted like I hadn't seen anything and walked round the mini-supermarket with a basket, taking my time, though I was expecting them to drop the security shutters at any moment.

I queued at one of three check-outs, the customer in front of me a man weighted down with a basket full of frozen meals. I glanced at him and he nodded cheerfully in return. In the other two queues people were chatting to one another or staring impatiently at the shop assistants to serve people even faster. They were good actors. Anybody passing through who didn't know the place wouldn't have known a thing.

That afternoon I avoided my replacement mother and stayed in my old room as if I were once more a recalcitrant teenager dodging the imputable risks of having to communicate with adults. It'd been two days since the scene at my father's funeral in which several distant relations had had to drag me away from the replacement mother. They'd corralled me into a corner of the back garden, telling me they understood grief made people do stupid things, but that I was scaring my mother. I mimicked calm and promised them I was feeling better. By early evening everybody but aunt Jean had left. She no longer had the indignant scowl of somebody convinced of their own moral turpitude, and if she was unafraid of leaving the replacement alone with me she never showed it.

Had she become one of them?

I sat in my room watching TV. I'd been scanning the news reports for the extraordinary, but there were as yet no obvious clues. I'd considered calling Adrianna to explain why I'd left Zielona Gora without speaking to her or the others, only when I thought about the replacements, I thought of her irreversibly altered. That frightened me even more than the replacement downstairs ensconced on a deck chair in the back garden sunning itself.

I was awake when the replacement mother finally went up to bed. I'd heard it crying earlier on, louder than the theme tune of the comedy show it'd been watching at the time, trying to draw me out. It was too late for more such trickery, for the inconceivable had become knowable to me.

I heard her treading along the landing, and so I slipped out of bed and flung the door open expecting her to be standing there listening. The landing was empty.

(16)

I'd learned nothing since leaving Zielona Gora tha explained how the replacements worked. Consistency o habit, strategy, even they way they acted wasn't entirel evident from what I'd observed. I'd no friends left in th village I trusted enough to even approach on those terms

108

MOUNTAINS OF SMOKE

The replacements, whether imitating old acquaintances or my mother, weren't overt in their transformation. If only the one in my parents' bedroom had in some way resembled a monster, at least that would have settled my feelings towards them.

I parked my father's old Land Rover at the side of the lane, unloaded the fishing tackle and climbed the steps to the reservoir. It was incredibly hot, and sweat stood out on the hairs on my arms. Through the barbed wire fence insects blotted the reservoir in dark clouds. I set up the rod, hooked the bait and cast the line out into the water. I didn't expect to catch anything, nor was I hoping to. I'd simply come out here to escape my replacement mother.

The emergence of more replacements had speeded up significantly, only it was no beautiful insect with dandelion colored wings pressing against the organic mesh of its pod, but something whose veins were dark with poison.

Wherever I went in the village they would follow me. At the very least they would tail me to the ends of their streets, pacing me on the opposite pavements. I knew many of the people, even if only to say hello to them. They would break-off at the corner of their streets as if instructed to go no further, only for somebody else to step out of their house and repeat the process. As far as I could see there was nobody else at the reservoir, but the trees were thick along its banks and anybody could have been hiding there.

The strangest aspect of remaining in Chapel Hill was that I'd grown into some kind of artificial comfort. They must have known that out in the towns and cities I'd have had no chance. Which made me all the more suspicious. Why had they so far left me alone? What were they planning? Whatever had happened to my father must have played some part in their decision.

I dangled my feet over the water. Flies occasionally hovered over me and I'd have to wave them away, only for them to return minutes later. Birds sometimes swooped down to the reservoir, perhaps mistaking themselves for hawks as they spied a glint of movement. All the time my line was slack in the water. Sometimes I'd hear a car on a country lane. I wished I was a kid again so I could explore the dank smelling foliage, and climb the trees.

How had they replaced my mother and all the others? This also threw up the one thing I hadn't really wanted to think about. Did the replacements absorb the mind from inside of the original body, or was the body perfectly replicated?

My father had been dead a month, and for each day that passed I was happier he wasn't here to witness the thing calling itself my mother parading round in her clothes like some grotesque model, uttering her noises, sleeping in their bed, as if it could replicate familiarity.

I was a defiant abnormality in the village, daring to exist among them, though I did not doubt there was some other face beneath the ones they wore that the replacements had yet to show me.

(17)

" ....*George, wake up...*"

I must have fallen asleep, for when I opened my eyes it was with the feeling that somebody was nearby and watching me. I sat up, my face burning from the sun. The sun was against them, flaring round their body. Was this it? They appeared to be undergoing some kind of spectacular conversion from one state to another. I'd caught them in th middle of their transformative act, seen them before they could get to me.

I jumped to my feet, but when the figure stepped towards me, I could see it was only the sun reflecting off the water which had made it seem like something it clearly wasn't.

"George?"

She'd dyed her hair red, into which she'd added streaks of black, as if they'd been mined rather than highlighted. She'd also lost some weight, and her brown eyes were restless, uncertain of what she was doing.

"Adrianna."

She took on a defeated look when I spoke, which I pictured her rehearsing with my replacement mother.

"...you'll have your work cut out for you..."

"...about this expression...?"

"It's me, George."

"Adrianna, all this way." I didn't modulate or try to improve on the flatness of my last one worded response at seeing her here.

The same look again, dejected I hadn't run to her.

"I was so sorry to hear about your father," she said.

She did look sorry, sad even.

"Probably for the best," I said.

"George, you don't mean that."

I walked over to her and despite myself slipped my arms round her. She smelled exactly like Adrianna had the day she'd sat next to me on the sofa in Toby's apartment. I thought about kissing her, that it'd be the best way to tell, but I pulled away before the image proved too strong for me to resist.

"Come for a drive with me."

She looked at me, not sure how she should proceed.

"If that's what you want."

"Of course."

"What about your fishing gear?"

I looked at the rod, which had been my father's.

"It's old and needs replacing."

Adrianna either didn't catch the meaning, or she really wasn't a replacement.

"Your mother dropped me off," she said, as we walked to the Land Rover.

"Where is she now?"

"I think she must have gone back home." There was hesitation in her voice. "George, aren't you going to ask what I'm doing here?"

I didn't look at her because she'd have perfected Adrianna's expression.

"I'm a bit lost for words."

"I didn't decide this lightly," she said.

We reached the Land Rover and she sat in the passenger seat, waiting for me to say something commendable.

"I should have told you why I had to leave, but I guess Julia must have told you I left a message on the school answer machine."

"It was Clive who told me to take a chance. I know the timing must seem awful to you."

I drove slowly along the deserted country lanes, only stooping trees peering over mossy walls, a tractor working it way up the furrows of its previous day's work.

"I bet he did?"

She looked at me funnily, but I didn't explain any further. We headed in the direction of the village, prepared to see replacements running out of the fields, animate scarecrows come to life, which in all likelihood I'd have found far less frightening.

It took us just under five minutes to reach what had been my parents' house.

"I forget something. Wait in the car, I'll only be a minute."

If she suspected anything, she didn't follow me.

I walked round the side of the house into the back garden where the replacement mother was pulling up weeds. A light perspiration covered the replacement's brow. She only heard me coming when my shadow fell over her. She lifted a hand to shield her eyes to see me properly, smiling, and for a moment she really did look like my mother.

(18)

I climbed back into the Land Rover to find Adrianna quietly watching the people in the street. One of the neighbors was mowing their lawn and two young girls were sitting on the pavement playing a game.

"I expected where you lived to be different."

I humored her, it was the least I could do under the circumstances.

"What were you hoping for?"

"I'm not really sure. Maybe something more bucolic."

I laughed, taken by surprise. A replacement with a sense of humor, when there was me thinking they were all so earnest.

"Let me guess, thatched cottages and horses clopping down the high street."

She laughed too, putting her hand on my forearm. Her palm was soft and warm and sweaty. I realized what game the two girls were playing. The pressure on my forearm increased.

"George?"

As I started the engine the girls stopped their game to watch us. Inadvertently they'd brought me back from the brink of giving myself over to the replacement in the passenger seat. If they'd had mobiles or tablets with them I might have succumbed to the Adrianna replacement. But the game they were playing was marbles, the anachronism breaking the spell.

"Just for show," I said.

"I don't understand?"

"I think you do."

I turned out of my parents street and onto one of the back roads that took us out of the village in record time. Solitary trees resembling arms bent at the elbow jabbed at the dry stone walls of the largest fields.

"Talk to me, George."

"I am talking to you."

"Let's go back to your mum's."

"What's wrong with you?"

She didn't answer.

"I'm leaving Chapel Hill," I said.

"I'm worried about you."

"Then come with me?"

"Let's go back," she repeated

"You came all this way and you don't want to come with me?"

In the rearview mirror a virulent expression blazed back at me. I'd thought about touching that face, kissing that mouth, but she was only a shaded in version of Adrianna, like something a child might produce in playschool. She was beguiling in simply being herself, in her physicality, but it wasn't enough to persuade me.

MOUNTAINS OF SMOKE

The lane hit a mile long stretch completely visible as it rode a series of small undulating hills. A vehicle was approaching from the opposite direction, the sky darkening behind it.

"George?" She gave a sigh as if I were beginning to bore her. "Where are you going?"

I'd only thought as far as the replacement mother. I hadn't considered they'd let me get any further.

The car ahead of us was a quarter of a mile nearer and looked like a taxi. I heard Adrianna unfasten the buckle of her seat belt. The sun had disappeared, clouds shadowing the vehicle.

Adrianna leaned across her seat and gently laid her hands on the steering wheel.

"Time to stop."

(19)

At first it was only a dark and nameless stretch of nowhere, a country lane in early evening, somehow strangely unrealized. I thought of a diagram, of measured lines leading into uncertainty. The wind blew theatrically through the forest, trees stirring, presaging what? My only hope was head trauma, irrevocable, absolving me of any responsibility. I opened my eyes, the gap so narrow it was as if somebody had stitched my lids together. Inexplicably, I remembered everything I didn't want to, the heat from the crash rising up through the tarmac like a warning of things to come. The Land Rover lay in a ditch on its side, its front wheels spinning, a competitor to my racing thoughts. Nearby a taxi-cab jutted from the trunk of a tree.

The replacement Adrianna stumbled out into the road, her bloodied head shuddering in the twilight haze which swam up her back and over shoulders, making a disheveled angel of her. She was screaming at the top of her voice, a strange sound, all the more comical for its falsetto, as if she'd engaged in the most ostentatious part of an Italian opera of large round people singing in high beautiful voices.

I looked down at the rock in my hands. Something wet and covered in clumps of bloodied hair stuck to the bottom of it. On the ground in front of me the driver of the taxi was dragging himself across the country lane. His legs made inward strokes against macadam, each foot finding purchase, propelling himself forward as if swimming imaginary lengths. He reached the roadside and crawled headfirst into a ditch. He was out of sight but I could hear him crying, hoping I wouldn't follow. I walked across the lane. He lay sprawled among the thick roots of a tree. When he looked up I imagined he saw something monstrous.

"You can't," he said, turning what remained of that part of his face towards me.

I had the rock above my head again, but this time I hesitated.

"Why?"

The replacement shrank back against the tree roots deliberately entangling himself so it would be difficult getting near him.

"Why?" I repeated.

The replacement looked at me.

"Because we're the same."

I thought about my grandmother and what she'd said about her brother, wondering if maybe they'd brought something back with them. Was it possible it had started not in Gijon or anywhere else, but here, in Chapel Hill?

"George, no."

I swung round and caught the replacement Adrianna in the side of the head with the rock. I heard something inside her skull crack open. She made a sound with her lips that sounded like...pffff. She fell into some bushes by the roadside making a shape like a human exclamation mark, and from beneath her head which blood spread outwards with dark viscous intensity.

I looked at the rock and the replacement taxi driver.

"I almost believed you."

A flap of skin fell away from the side of his face, part of his jawbone revealed.

"Are you scared?" I asked.

He nodded.

"Good, you should be."

Made in the USA
Columbia, SC
05 May 2021